D1575651

**Donated By :**

Rita Hawes

To: _____     From: _____

# Heavenly
# Patchwork II

*Quilt Stories to Warm Your Heart*

by Judy Howard

Dorcas Publishing, Oklahoma City, OK
www.heavenlypatchwork.com

# *Endorsements for Heavenly Patchwork II*

"This is the perfect book with which to curl up with a hot cup of tea and enjoy all the heart-warming stories by women like us. We each have a story to tell, and each of these stories delivers a message of comfort." **Esterita Austin**, www.esteritaaustin.com,

"Once again, *Heavenly Patchwork II* rewards us with meaningful stories that evoke the real meaning of quiltmaking. The stitches go beyond just design and piecing to finding a place in our homes and hearts." **Georgia J. Bonesteel** author of *Georgia Bonesteel's Quiltmaking Legacy*, www.georgiabonesteel.com

"*Heavenly Patchwork II* gives me as a quilting teacher pause to reflect on my humanly gifts of grace, forgiveness, and redemption while stitching. The stories are poignantly uplifting and worthy of Howard's efforts to minister in her special way." **Linda Carlson**, author, www.lindacarlsonquilts.com

"*Heavenly Patchwork II* from Judy Howard is a feel-good book full of heart-warming stories that bind all quilters into a patchwork of love and caring. You'll want to read this book again and again!" **Kathy Delaney**, www.kathydelaney.com, author of: *Hearts and Flowers - Hand Appliqué, A Heartland Album, The Basics - An Easy Guide to Beginning Quiltmaking, Horn of Plenty,* and *Patterns of History.*

"Another winner from Judy Howard of Buckboard Quilts! Good reading for a quiet evening." **Helen Kelley**, author of *Every Quilt Tells a Story* and *Helen Kelley's Joy of Quilting*, www.helenkelley-patchworks.com

"When they count quilting angels in heaven they'll have to include Judy Howard who has pulled together another collection of heart-warming stories of quilts, quilters and the good they bring to the world. *Heavenly Patchwork II* is a must for everyone who loves quilting. Best of all, the profits go to support charity quilt projects throughout the country to keep the love cycling through the lives of people who receive these hand-made blessings. **Nancy Kirk**, quilt designer, appraiser, author and lecturer, www.kirkcollection.com

"Once again, renowned quilt dealer Judy Howard shares a collection of heartwarming stories told by quilters themselves. We know that quilts give us comfort; how much more so when we hear from those who made them! These personal essays are sure to touch your spirit. Curl up under your favorite quilt and enjoy this comforting read." **Rhonda Richards**, editor of *Great American Quilts* book series.

"Readers will enjoy true-life stories of compassion, love and friendship in this second collection, *Heavenly Patchwork.*" ***Jan Krentz,*** quilt teacher, author, and designer. (Box 686 Poway, CA 92074)

# Contents

## *Comfort Quilts*

## Healing Quilts

## Memorial Quilts

# Faith Quilts

*Dedicated to quilters everywhere, past and present, who capture and preserve our history through their quilts.*

# Acknowledgements

Creating *Heavenly Patchwork II* has been an exciting challenge made possible and enjoyable by the many companions who have helped along this journey. My heartfelt gratitude and thanks to:

My loving husband Bill who encouraged me. Family and friends who faithfully prayed, advised, read and edited the stories: Chalise Miner, Gayla White, Kathryn Fanning, M.J. Van Deventer, M. Carolyn Steele, Kay Bishop, Carolyn Leonard, Melba Lovelace, Judi Malarkey, Beverly Sievers, Delaine Gately, Rhonda Richards, Laura Palmer, Dr. Don and Janet Addison, Penny and Brenda Addison, Bill and JoAnn Jones, Marsha Mueller, Deborah Johnson, Janis Montgomery Contway, Faye Ham, Sandy See, Lori Hall, Jacque Rutledge, Maria Veres, Lynette Bennett, Jodi Brungardt, Darlina Eichman, Danelle Hall, Dee Anne Heaton, Pam Kozak, Dee Nash, Mary Price, Kristyn Reid, Rebecca Robison, Barbara Shepherd, Michelle Metcalfe, Metropolitan Libraries.

Harn Homestead & 1889'er Museum, Canadian County Historical Museum, National Cowboy & Western Heritage Museum, Mildred Heitzke, Bea Kimbrough, Sandra Kadavy, David and Cheryl K. Merritt, Mildred Dillard, Millicent Gillogly, Ruth Harris, Don Lusk, Zolalee Gaylor, Karen Judd, Gary Wasson, Jim Gatling, Adrian Thompson, Joe Galusha, Lisa Foley, Scope Ministries, Intl., Oklahoma Baptist University, Oklahoma Historical Society, Marcia Hohn of quilterscache.com for photo settings and quilts, master artist Bob Annesley for Mary's Sunshine, Keith Rinearson for cover photo, Darlene and Charlie Rook for cover quilt and setting, Gayla White, AGlimpsePhotography.com, for the layout, graphics and cover design.

To everyone who submitted their heart-warming true stories. And most importantly to my heavenly Father who directed me in compiling these stories to inspire women to look to Him for their source of joy, strength, comfort and healing.

Preserve your priceless family heritage by sharing your quilt story. Email your 50-700 word story to BuckboardQuilts@cox.net, or mail to:
12101 N. MacArthur, Suite 137
Oklahoma City, OK 73162-1800
or call 405-751-3885
See www.HeavenlyPatchwork.com for writing guidelines.
See www.BuckboardQuilts.com for 200 quilts.

# The Impossible Dream

## by Judy Howard

My teachers in the 1950s and 60s cataloged me as a half-wit and socially retarded because I was so shy. Now educators have a kinder explanation—severe dyslexia and disadvantaged. I struggled through high school and college, graduating only because of my bull-dogged tenacity. At age sixty, I enrolled in my first computer and writing classes and prayed for divine intervention. Still the writing came hard for me. The computer classes contributed only major adrenal stress and migraines. I began doubting God's dream to write quilt stories about women who had pieced their brokenness into beauty by believing Him.

\*\*\*

Eleven months after God revealed His dream, *Heavenly Patchwork—Quilt Stories Stitched with Love* rolled off the press. Seven months later I'd sold 6000 books, ordered another 5000 books, received seven awards, been interviewed by ABC, NBC, CBS, PBS, COX, CNN, Oklahoma radio, newspapers and magazines — and I'm half finished with a second book.

\*\*\*

"I'm sorry . . . I have bad news for you on reprinting *Heavenly Patchwork I*," Kathy, the production manager at the printers, told me. "Your job has been printed and will be bound today—but we found a mistake on the Title Page. I don't know how it could have happened, but Dorcas Publishing is misspelled. What do you want to do? As it is, we can't get the books delivered for another week. And if we make the correction, it delays it another month."

Besides Hobby Lobby, I had people desperate to get their backordered books in time for Christmas sales and it was now two weeks later than the promised delivery date. With six book signings scheduled and only a few books on hand, what could I do but accept the mistake. "I'll call this my Devil's Eye—my act of humility because only God can create perfection," I told my husband through tears. "The quilters will understand."

I was wrong when I thought nothing more could go wrong that week. After the computer temporarily crashing and waiting for the professional photographer's cover photo for *Heavenly Patchwork II*, I discovered that the shot wouldn't work. "Where are you, God?" I screamed in anger and frustration.

Sinking into deep despair with deadlines looming, I fell to my knees and pleaded for a new idea. Graciously God brought to mind several antique collector friends with homes designed as 1700s colonial masterpieces. After a few more futile attempts shooting the cover photo sending me into emotional roller-coaster rides, God finally provided the perfect quilt and fireplace to cover His second book at Darlene and Charlie Rook's home.

When I asked Darlene about the quilt, she replied, "In 1967, my mother Lorene Leary made this beautiful Oak Leaf and Reel appliqué. I entered it in the Oklahoma State Fair, and since it was Mother's first and only attempt at quilt-making, we were shocked when it won third place.

"Mother was so stunned when I presented her the ribbon she cried and then apologized, 'Oh, honey, if I'd known you were going to enter it, I'd have done a better job. I never told you about accidentally knocking a lamp over and burning the center square the day before I gave it to you. I stayed up all night repairing it. Can't believe the judges didn't disqualify it.'

"Since Mom passed away shortly after, her quilt is even more precious."

***

Often while compiling these stories and rushing from book signings to quilt exhibits and programs, I pause to ask myself an important question. Is my spiritual blanket of love becoming threadbare from misplaced priorities? Is my eternal quilt evolving haphazardly, pieced from prideful, selfish or shortsighted desires? Or is the fabric of my life permanently appliquéd onto the foundation of Jesus' sacrificial love, stitched in utter dependence to His grace, mercy and guidance? What legacy will I leave?

God works in mysterious ways. And sometimes He stretches my faith to the breaking point. My prayer for you is that you don't give up. Keep trusting God for the victory He promises when you commit your way to Him. And pray, already believing. He will carry you through your daily trials, give you new eyes to see His eternal perspective and shift your focus to praising Him for His unchanging love. He does it for me time and again, in such surprising (and sometimes last minute) ways.

*"My grace is sufficient for you.*
*My Strength is made perfect in weakness . . .*
*Therefore most gladly I will rather boast in my infirmities,*
*that the power of Christ may rest upon me."*
*2 Corinthians 12:9*

---

Copy and mail the **ORDER FORM** on Page 182 for gifts for friends and family or for fund-raising. All book profits provide quilts for children and families in crisis situations. Your support makes a difference.

X

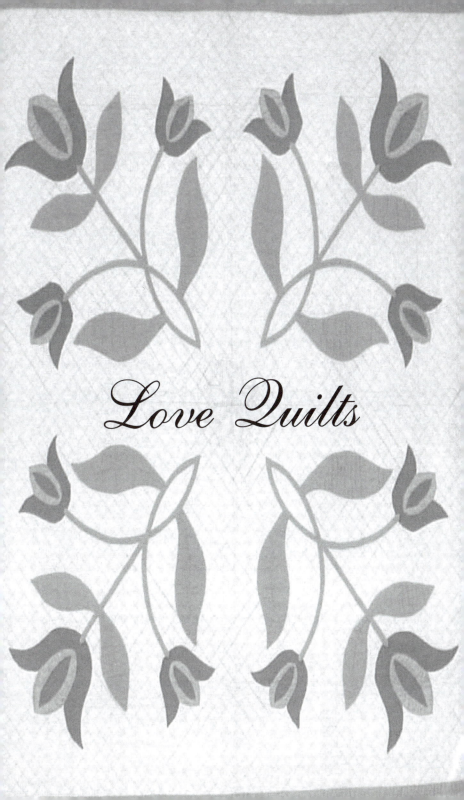

Love Quilts

# *Healing the Broken Heart*

### *Letter written to Judy Howard*

Dear Mrs. Howard, I'm writing this letter to thank you.

Ten years ago in a fit of rage and intentional cruelty, my ex-husband burned all my family heirloom quilts from my great-grandmother. He even burned her quilting frames.

I told my boyfriend John of my ex-husband's numerous cruel acts and couldn't stop weeping when I lamented about my irreplaceable quilts. Over the past seven years we've dated, John had proposed many times and I'd continually turned him down— the Queen of Excuses. In a heated argument, John asked me why I kept putting off getting married. Finally, I confessed that after my first experience, I didn't think I ever could get married. How could I possibly open myself up to someone else and risk being hurt again? How could I learn to trust anyone again with my heart and what precious belongings I still had?

Then on December 12, 2005, John called saying he was coming over to give me my birthday and Christmas present early. Little did I know that he had discovered the "perfect gift" that would melt the ice in my heart.

John shooed me out of my bedroom while he carefully arranged his gifts for maximum impact. Then he gently took my hands and whispered, "Before I let you see your presents, I want you to know that these are not intended to replace what you've lost. But if you can bring yourself to trust me, I hope they'll adequately express that I would give the world to make your life whole again."

John opened the door and I immediately burst into tears of joy and screamed at the sight of three quilts of exquisite beauty spread out on my bed. I was amazed that John could be so caring and compassionate in giving of himself to ease my pain. I didn't realize how angry and bitter I had become until his gift of love broke down the protective barriers I'd erected around my soul. Those quilts and his kind act restored my faith in people and gave me hope.

John also handed me a copy of your *Heavenly Patchwork* book which I have to keep putting down, because I've done nothing but cry tears of joy while reading it. The stories are such a wonderful inspiration. So once again, I must say thank you for your part in bringing healing to my hardened heart through your quilts and book.

***

This letter was in response to John's visit to Buckboard Quilts located in my home. After making his list and checking it twice, having studied my website, John made excellent choices. He was on a focused mission and couldn't contain his excitement. Parting with Emmajean's Roses and Bows appliqué (in "Emmajean's Lifelong Passion" story) that was also pictured on the title and chapter pages for *Heavenly Patchwork I* and the Mennonite Tulip appliqué that is on this book's title and chapter pages was like saying

farewell to old friends. John selected only the best, including the irreplaceable mint unwashed navy Double Irish Chain from the 1800s. Never have I seen such tender-hearted kindness and sensitivity as John demonstrated.

*"If you then, being evil,*
*know how to give good gifts to your children,*
*how much more will your Father who is in heaven*
*give good things to those who ask Him!"*
*Matthew 7:11*

# Something Special

### by M. Carolyn Steele

"You have to do it, Mom. I'm at my wit's end." Traci plumps down in my easy chair, her belly round with my first grandchild, and gives an exasperated sigh.

"You're just hot and tired, honey. I'll take you shopping again tomorrow."

She rolls her eyes at me, so I offer, "Even buy you lunch."

"Thank you, Mom, but we've already looked everywhere," she reminds me. "Besides, the quilts are starting to look alike, blocks and bunnies and teddy bears." She leans forward and her hazel eyes drill a hole in me. "I don't want this baby to have something ordinary. Don't you understand? You're the only one who can make it special."

I can feel my resolve dissolve and I know I'm going to falter. I try to bite my tongue, but how do you say no to a daughter who thinks you can do anything, who thinks you're superwoman? How do you tell her you've just been lucky, something always has guided your fingers or whispered the right thing to do?

Traci sinks back into the cushions, pushing damp curls from her face and smiles. It is the same smile that has warmed my heart for thirty years.

"Yes, I understand," I say. And, I mean it. This child's crib blanket has to be special. It has to mean something. This is my first grandchild. A boy, they tell me, who will be called Cameron.

Relief widens Traci's smile, pushing dimples deep in her cheeks as I nod and give back the smile, a silent acceptance of the task.

But the task is larger than I realize. "Special" doesn't come easy. I worry around with fabrics and designs, scouring the recesses of my mind for an idea. I'd like to say the thought comes like a thunderbolt, but it doesn't. It comes in bits and pieces as I ponder the coming boy-child, wishing my mother could have lived to see him, remembering the progression of our family from Poland and her pride in their accomplishments.

I think my fingers knew first what the design would be, knew that the sketch of the tall sailing ship that carried my great-grandfather and his parents to our shores would find its way onto the quilt. The water forever would beckon the ancestor who changed his last name to sound more American. He would make his living sailing the Great Lakes and, then, during the Gold Rush era, he would take his son, my mother's father, and ply the waters off Alaska. Descendants are still there, yet today, making their living aboard boats.

My project, crowded with these memories, takes shape with each stitch of the needle. Wind billows layers of patterned sails on a wooden ship. The ocean that inhabits the bottom of the small quilt comes to life with a pod of whales and clouds share a cheerful sky with seagulls. The arrival of distant ancestors lives in the quilt as a lighthouse stands sentinel over the tranquil sea and welcomes immigrants to its shores.

I allow myself a bit of pride as I hand over the finished quilt at Traci's baby shower—pride in my accomplishment, pride in the ancestry that inspired the effort. But this moment is tempered with a tiny worry.

"Do you like it, honey? I know it doesn't exactly have any baby colors, but you said you wanted something different. And, the ocean is so much a part of our history."

"Oh, Mom," Traci murmurs. "I love it." She struggles to lift herself from the chair and allows the quilt to unfold, revealing the entire scene. "It's just what I wanted for the baby's crib. It's something special, something just for Cameron."

*"You knit me together in my mother's womb. I praise You, because I am fearfully and wonderfully made; Your works are wonderful . . . All the days ordained for me were written in Your book before one of them came to be." Psalm 139:13b-16*

## Quilt Bathed in Tears

*as told by Ginger Van Horn to Judy Howard*

I have three quilts made during the Civil War, but one holds a secret place in my heart. It was made by my great-great-great aunt Mary Elisabeth Weaver.

Mary Elisabeth was engaged to a young man who valiantly marched off to war. They were to be married immediately after his homecoming. Tragically, her fiancé was killed and never returned. Distraught, Mary Elisabeth cut up her wedding dress into tiny squares and created a quilt out of the dress. During those times, brides wore colored calico dresses, not white like our custom now.

Every time I touch Mary Elisabeth's quilt, I imagine how many tears bathed her quilt as she worked through her grief and sorrow.

*"He heals the brokenhearted and binds up their wounds."*
*Psalm 147:3*

# Endless Chain

*as told by Shirley Randle*
*to Judy Howard*

Shirley Williams Randle joined the Spinning Spool Quilt Guild in Shawnee, Oklahoma in 1990, the same year she started making a wedding quilt for her daughter. When Shirley traveled to Cushing to nurse her ailing father, she took the quilt to work on.

Born in 1907, the year Oklahoma became a state, Harbon Carter Robinson blinked back tears and said, "That quilt brings a flood of memories. When I was a kid, I helped Mother lower the frame from the ceiling in the homestead her parents claimed in the Land Run of 1889." Harbon's mother and grandmother spent winter evenings quilting in front of the fireplace. They made the family's bedding to keep them warm.

Harbon told Shirley, "Knowing how much I loved quilts, Mom made a Bear Paw quilt just for me." The quilt was especially meaningful to him since his mother died when Harbon was fifteen, leaving him an orphan. "The sheriff auctioned the family farm and the contents to settle the estate debts — including my Bear Paw," Harbon said. "It broke my heart because that was my only tangible reminder of Mom." Harbon was left with only his saddle which he had buried in the woods.

Recently, Shirley visited her niece Diana in Houston. Together they attended the International Quilt Show and Diana got hooked on quilting. The first quilt she made was a Bear Paw. When Shirley told her about her grandfather Harbon's Bear Paw quilt that the sheriff sold, Diana burst into tears. The cycle of his mother's love had continued in an unspoken endless chain through three generations with a little divine intervention.

*"For the LORD is good;*
*His mercy is everlasting,*
*and His truth endures to all generations."*
*Psalm 100:5*

## *Hydro's World's Fair*

*as told by Lucille Ralstom to Judy Howard*

"Yaah. A jeans quilt would be way cool, Grandma. Just don't put any fuzzies on my quilt," was Lucille's grandson's reply when asked what kind of quilt he'd like for his bed.

So Lucille Ralston began work on the first of four scrappy jean quilts she made for her four grandchildren. She embellished them with machine embroidery and tacked them with machined teardrops in variegated colored thread instead of yarn fuzzies.

Lucille always has been innovative and creative in her quilt-making. For instance, she designed a heart-shaped wall hanging with the fan pattern for the bottom half and random crazy patching for the top. She attached her mom's and grandmom's necklaces, bracelets, earrings, keys and rings as a clever keepsake for gifts to eight lucky family members last Christmas.

In another novel project, Lucille cut two inch circles out of her mom's old dresses. She set them together with solid yellow YoYos surrounding each group of seven calico circles and made them into YoYo wall hangings for the next Christmas' gifts.

The cousins loved Lucille's Christmas Tree quilt she made to be auctioned off at the family reunion one summer. She had designed her own pattern by enlarging a Christmas tree picture she found on a grocery sack. After piecing the tree together, she appliquéd packages at the bottom with family name tags ironed on with sticky adhesive.

She even painstakingly appliquéd candy cane ornaments on the branches with even more family names penned on. That quilt won the prize for earning the most money ever to fund the cost of renting a room and catering the family reunions held each year.

The year before Lucille, passed out star blocks to the women at the reunion and had them embroider their family names on each block. She pieced enough squares together to make two tops which she then hand-quilted. She auctioned one off at the reunion and kept the other for her husband Jerry, recently diagnosed with Lou Gehrigs Disease.

Lucille learned to quilt at age four during quilting bees while she was playing beneath her grandmother Julia's frame on the farm Julia and Claiborne King had homesteaded between Binger and Eakly, Oklahoma in the 1890s. Lucille mimicked the women of the Oakdale Thimble Club by poking her needle up and down through the quilt. The Kings were peanut and cotton farmers and attended the Oakdale Baptist Church on Highway 152 which was the social center of the small farming community.

Lucille started quilting in earnest in high school when she created her hand-painted state bird and flower quilt. For a wedding gift, Jerry's mom Flossie gave them the wool Crazy quilt dated 1916 which her mother-in-law Virginia Pennington Ralston had made as a wedding gift for Pete and Flossie. When Lucille received her first electric blanket, she foolishly gave the Crazy quilt back to her in-laws. Much to Lucille's delight, Flossie returned the Crazy to her son twenty years later.

Since Lucille worked for twenty-six years doing alterations in Weatherford, she had an overflowing scrap bag from which to make the one hundred or more quilts she's sewn in the last fifty years. Four albums, one for each of her grandchildren, bulge with pictures of those quilts, the stories behind each, and the names of the eventual recipient. Just recently, Lucille completed sewing a label to each quilt.

Though she's too humble to enter her quilts in contests, her children have submitted Lucille's quilts in the Hydro World's Fair and brought home lots of blue ribbons.

"Grandpa, it's not really the World's Fair . . . is it?" Jerry's eight-year-old grandson asked.

"Naw. But that's what I call it because you see everyone in the world you've ever known at the Hydro County Fair," Jerry explained.

> *"And whatever you do, do it heartily,*
> *as to the Lord and not to men,*
> *knowing that from the Lord*
> *you will receive the reward of the inheritance;*
> *for you serve the Lord Christ."*
> *Colossians 3:23-24*

# An Extravagance of Silk

### by M. Carolyn Steele

Lilly Steele leaned slightly in her chair to watch her son Arthur stand outside and shake rain from his overcoat. Lately, her accumulation of years stirred old memories. She'd already passed the allotted three-score and ten the Lord promised.

Maybe it was just the winter weather that occasioned recollections of her marriage in Indian Territory and the family's nomadic life following coal mining jobs — living in shacks where wind found its way between cracks and stirred the curtains of closed windows. The only way to keep warm was to sit bundled in a heavy quilt.

She rubbed the calluses on her index and middle fingers with her thumb, remembering the tedium of piecing various shaped fabric blocks by the light of a coal-oil lantern. Utility quilts, that's what they were—meant for heavy use, fashioned from scraps of worn clothing.

The back door opened and Arthur bustled into the kitchen.

With a shiver, Lilly stretched forward to let down the oven door. A warmth, heavy with the aroma of the day's baking bread, enveloped her. She propped her leather-clad feet on the open door.

"Evenin', Ma." Arthur grinned.

"Evenin', son." He did look nice in his bus driver's uniform. Thank heavens the mines wouldn't be taking any more of the lives and limbs of her men folk. She allowed only a brief feeling of pride. Wouldn't do to dwell on good fortune. Pride goeth before destruction.

Arthur pulled a chair from the table and settled himself in front of the oven. "What's gone on today?" He glanced at the loaves of bread turned out on the cabinet. "Where's Georgia? She reckon to take a holiday from fixin' supper?"

"No," Lilly answered, concealing a smile. "She's gone to tell Ethel the news."

"News? 'Bout what?" Arthur shook a cigarette from a half-empty package. "I can't reckon on what could be more important than supper." He flicked a match to life.

"That so?" Happiness twitched at the corner of her lips. "Well then, I guess you reckon your belly to be more important than the fact you and her is due to be grandparents come summer."

"What?" Arthur looked up, the unlit cigarette dangling from his lower lip.

"It be a fact." Lilly succumbed to the smile. Such joy couldn't be held in for long.

"Well, I'll be—" Flames crawled along the match and he quickly lit the cigarette. "A grandbaby."

"You think there's another quilt left in me?" Lilly held both hands up, knuckles gnarled like boles on a tree. "A little quilt, just the right size for a baby."

"Sure, Ma. Make it a pretty one this time. None of those old dress scraps. I reckon we can find money for new material." He snapped his fingers. "Silk! It ought to be blue silk."

"Silk? Ain't that an extravagance, Arthur?"

"Only the best for my grandson."

"Might be a girl," Lilly insisted. "Wouldn't hurt to buy a length of pink silk, too."

***

Lilly permitted a bit of self-satisfaction as she eyed the baby quilt wrapped around her great-grandson. Her fingers knew the soul of the silk—the weight, the feel, how the smooth surfaces slipped across each other as she hand-stitched the pink and blue squares into a checkerboard pattern. It was, indeed, a wonderful extravagance.

She watched Georgia cuddle the toddler on her lap at the opposite end of the sofa. Little Carl massaged the lustrous silk with one hand, intent on the stories woven by his grandmother about the tiny angels that populated the flannel backing. They swung from stars and sat in the curve of crescent moons. Eyes heavy, he nestled into the quilt.

With a sigh, Lilly closed her eyes, too, and folded her hands in her lap. They ached with a lifetime of labor. The Lord gave her a talent. Surely, He was pleased with her last effort.

***

"It's sixty-two years old," Carl said as he surveyed the shredded silk covering on his baby quilt.

"No wonder it's a tad worn," his wife murmured and spread the quilt out.

Carl folded the corner over to expose the flannel underneath. "The back is in good shape. See the angels? Grandma called them Winkin', Blinkin', and Nod." He sighed, "Couldn't we just make a new top? I'd like our grandson to have something made by his three-great-grandmother."

"Yes, I suppose—"

"Silk." He patted the faded squares. "Let's make it silk."

*"And my God shall supply all your need according to His riches in glory by Christ Jesus." Philippians 4:19*

# Tobacco Sacks at Church?

*as told by Clara Schoeck's grandchildren to Judy Howard*

Clara Schoeck was married at age seventeen in a tiny church in Adair, Oklahoma in 1934. When Clara's first baby was born a year later, the ladies of the church wanted to surprise Clara with a Flower Basket quilt for her daughter. The only problem was that nobody had the money to buy fabric.

"I've stashed away some old tobacco sacks," volunteered one lady, a little embarrassed to admit. "I could dye them pink."

"We could use the pink calico dress I've outgrown," another suggested.

"And I've got some C&H Sugar Sacks I've been saving for a special quilt."

"My husband has a WWI airplane cover stored in the barn we could use for the backing." another volunteered.

"We've picked enough cotton that I could card for the batting," the farmer's daughter offered.

The next week, they brought their sacks, scraps, airplane cover and cotton bats along with their lunches to church. The needles started flying.

"Let's embroider our names on the blocks and maybe in the middle we could say, 'To Baby with love, 1935' " brainstormed one of the quilters.

"How about writing our favorite Bible verses on the handle of each basket?" another chimed in.

Two months later, the quilting group presented the quilt to Clara, which astonished and delighted her. "Where did you find such beautiful fabrics in this day and age?" Clara inquired.

With a sly giggle, the spokeswoman explained, "Where God guides, God also provides."

Nellie cherishes her Flower Basket quilt to this day and loves to share the story of how faithful God was and still is to provide for their needs. "The legacy of God's love is embodied in every stitch," she said. "The verse on each handle is etched in the minds of my children. As I tucked them into bed each night, we repeated the verses together until they fell into a peaceful slumber."

> *"Train up a child in the way he should go,*
> *and when he is old, he will not depart from it."*
> *Proverbs 22:6*

# Jake's Quilt

*by Rebecca Holmberg Freeman*

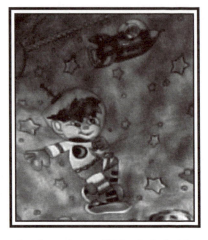

My house bursts with shrill noise, but I don't care. There's big doin's today. It's Jake's seventh birthday. My great-nephew is already celebrating. An Oklahoma tornado has been unleashed in my front yard. My antique school bell—the back-up for my doorbell—loudly rings. We cover our ears until Gail can haul our boy off his chair-ladder.

Cake, ice cream, and a chorus of "Happy Birthday" give way to my present of wooden building blocks. The blocks are quickly piled up, only to fall down again with a noisy clatter. But wait. There's one more present hidden in my sewing room trunk. Jake leads the race as we hurry to find the treasure.

The scarred trunk was painted and decorated by my father. Jake helps me lift the heavy lid, and a magic aroma floats into the air.

"What's that funny smell, Aunt B? It makes my nose itch."

"That's history, Jake. My mother, grandmothers, and Aunt Edith are talking to us."

I balance an old three-generation photograph on the trunk's lid. My mother, just Jake's age, and my grandmother stare solemnly at us.

We search deeper into this mysterious box of adventure. Mesmerized by the bright patterns and fabric colors, Jake touches the swirling designs and fuzzy seam allowances of a quilt top. *Surprise!* I turn the fabric over and tiny blocks sewn together with precision and pride explode into beautifully crafted interlocking wedding rings. I explain that quilts are just like family. Unlike falling wooden blocks, these pieces are meant to stay together.

My mother's wedding quilt top is as beautiful as she was on her wedding day. It's finished, except for one block, carefully wrapped in yellowing tissue paper. Granny Robbins kept a cautious distance from needle and thread, but she tried to sew for my mother. Love is not always perfect. Recognizing love's effort is what really counts.

Suddenly, eager fingers reach for a small quilt covering a doll once owned by my brother, Jake's very own papa. I show him my picture, captured in Kodak time, when I dropped the doll and broke her foot. Jake checks it out. Yep, it's taped together.

"That's really you?"

"Yep. And that little boy in the picture is your papa."

Blue eyes grow big as Jake considers the proof before him.

"It's true! He really did wear the jumper suit you see on the doll."

He'll give it some thought. A guy has to watch out for Aunt B and her funny stories.

I rescue a picture of Grandma St. Clair taken the day she gave me my "big girl" quilt. See? Here's fabric from my favorite blouse, sewn by Aunt Edith, and trimmed with rhinestone buttons.

But, what's this? There's one quilt left in the trunk.

"Look, Jake. I see a shooting star with your name on it, and 'Planet Number Seven' in honor of your seventh birthday."

"I see it! I *see* it!"

"Look at the astronaut and the puppy dog piloting the flying saucer. There's a space ship with 'USA#1' on the side. Is that you at the controls?"

Jake is instantly in orbit, "Yes. It's me. Look, momma. It's *me*."

The other children whisper, "*Cool!*"

With a last backward glance, I smile contentedly and silently close the sewing room door. It's been a long day for our birthday boy. He's fast asleep under his own "big boy" quilt, dreaming of places we can't travel.

But I won't worry about Jake. We're linked together throughout time. Every family pieces its own story; each child contributes a uniquely perfect pattern. God is the Master Quilter, and we are part of His grand design.

*"The everlasting God, the LORD,*
*the Creator of the ends of the earth,*
*neither faints nor is weary.*
*His understanding is unsearchable.*
*He gives power to the weak,*
*and to those who have no might He increases strength . . .*
*those who wait on the LORD shall renew their strength;*
*they shall mount up with wings like eagles . . ."*
*Isaiah 40:28b-29, 31*

# *Mrs. Pinky Quilts for Halves*

### *by Judy Howard*

Born in 1913, Lydia Pinky worked for Elnora Jane Peabody in segregated Watonga, Oklahoma during the depression. Lydia loved to quilt after working hard all day performing the back-breaking chores of cleaning, cooking, gardening, canning and raising her mistress's children.

One day, Mrs. Pinky brought over to share a State Bird and Sunbonnet Sue quilt to comfort, cheer and entertain Elnora's children who had the measles. The children were delighted and Mrs. Peabody was impressed with the fine stitching, bright colors and artistic genius exhibited in Lydia's beautiful quilts.

"Would you make some quilts for me?" Elnora asked. "I'd love to have one for each child as a keepsake and one for my niece who's getting married in June." Lydia graciously agreed.

One spring morning, Elnora entertained her bridge club with brunch and showed the quilts to her friends. Each lady requested that Lydia make a quilt for her, and an idea began to formulate. Elnora, being the opportunist that she was, proposed the perfect plan to Lydia. "If you'll make the quilts, I'll sell them for you to my friends. We can go 'halves' and split the money." Thus began a long-lasting business arrangement between Mrs. Pinky and Mrs. Peabody.

At every tea, coffee, fund-raiser and social event Elnora hosted or attended, she displayed Lydia's quilts, which were greatly admired and quickly purchased by the women of Watonga.

Though Lydia never personally received the glory or attention for her workmanship, it will live on as a legend and tribute to a Godly woman who served humbly as unto the Lord.

> *"Bondservants, be obedient to those who are your masters . . .*
> *as bondservants of Christ,*
> *doing the will of God from the heart . . .*
> *doing service, as to the Lord, and not to men,*
> *knowing that whatever good anyone does,*
> *he will receive the same from the Lord,*
> *whether he is a slave or free."*
> *Ephesians 6:6-8*

## Go Derek

*as told by Betty Hennesy*
*to Judy Howard*

"Go Derek" read the caption under the picture of the ten-year-old black belt karate grandson of Betty Hennesy. The picture appeared in Oklahoma Quiltworks' newsletter in Oklahoma City where Derek, along with ten little girls, took a quilting class.

No strangers to quilting, Derek and his grandmother spent one summer cutting out two-inch squares to make a quilt together. After reading every quilt book in the Antlers, Oklahoma library where his mom was librarian, Derek loved arranging the different colored calicos to fit together into an artistic quilt.

Downsizing after her husband's death last Christmas, Betty gave Derek her Bernina sewing machine along with fabrics he personally chose from her vast stash.

"Where did you find all this fabric, Grandma?" Derek asked, amazed after going through the 8'x10' air-conditioned room in the garage and one bedroom stacked floor to ceiling with material, patterns, and books.

Betty explained that her collection represented a lifetime of collecting cloth on every trip she and her husband took in Europe and the United States. "This Liberty of London silky cotton that I bought in England is my favorite," she told Derek. "I brought back a whole suitcase full." After Betty gets her cataracts removed, she plans to make a quilt from an indigo and white pattern which belonged to one Budapest family clan. And would you believe, once, while everyone else toured the famous cathedrals in Paris, Betty shopped for material at LaRavay. "I must have made a lasting impression on the quilt shop owner since she recognized me at the Houston Quilt Show years later." Betty chuckled.

Betty admitted that her fabrics were the hardest things to part with because they reminded her of every trip she and her husband took together.

Derek wondered how his grandmother started quilting.

Here's the story Betty told Derek:

"When my grandmother Maggie Petty was about your age, her parents brought her to Oklahoma in a covered wagon. They homesteaded in Oklahoma City where 16th and North McArthur is today. Maggie taught me to quilt and always told me, 'If you don't have time to do it right, don't do it at all.'" Betty showed Derek the Dutch Doll quilt that she inherited in 1952 when her own grandma died suddenly from a heart attack.

Betty's husband never appreciated quilting until Betty brought home a Texas Star from the Clarita Amish Auction. Her husband immediately claimed it for himself and wanted it on his bed at all times. "I can't bear to part with it. I'll take it with me when I move to The Waterford Mansion along with my Sunbonnet Sue and this Dahlia."

Betty explained that while traveling through Mesa, Arizona, she spotted a "Quilts for Sale" sign and pulled in. An old-maid school teacher showed her a gorgeous quilt that the teacher's nieces and nephews were fighting over. Not knowing how to settle the family squabble, the teacher sold the Dahlia quilt to Betty. Since one niece had told her, "Aunt Elsie, you can't take it with you when you die," Elsie did the next best thing. She asked Betty to make her check out to the Lutheran Church.

Derek told his grandma that her passion for fabric and quilting must be in his blood. "I could spend hours playing with this neat stuff. I'm hopelessly hooked on quilting, thanks to you," Derek said as he hugged his grandma.

*"'You shall love the LORD your God with all your heart . . .'"*
*Matthew 22:29*

## Perils of Quilt Shopping in Iowa
### by Judy Howard

"I heard about an Amish quilt shop fifty miles north of here. Let's go check it out," Linda Marie said, anxious to escape the demands of her three preschool girls and everyday life in Mt. Pleasant, Iowa.

"Sounds great!" I said and grabbed my jacket. "I'm always ready for an adventure. I hoped we'd find time for some antiquing and quilt shopping while we were visiting you."

Off we drove, stopping at every antique shop along the way. Linda found an adorable oak drop-front secretary, perfect for her guest bedroom. At the next stop she found a small cherry Victorian dresser that matched her grandmother's bedroom set which she had just inherited. We squeezed it in and proceeded on our journey.

"Hey, I thought I was the antique dealer, and you're finding the good stuff," I kidded. About then we spotted the quilt shop sign and pulled up next to the farmhouse. There was a peculiar odor when we stepped out that about knocked us over. "What's this, a pig farm or something?" Linda giggled.

We rapped on the door and were greeted by a pleasant Amish lady, wearing her starched white cap and apron over her bright blue dress. She ushered us down to her basement shop with shelves lined with hundreds of bolts of fabric and a bed stacked high with quilts. The Sunshine and Shadow quilt immediately caught my eye. I loved

its dramatic solid wool crepe fabrics of purple, lavender, periwinkle and soft robin's egg blue. "This is the most stunning graphic work of art I've ever seen." I exclaimed. "How old is it and who made it?"

"My grandmother made this for my mother's wedding gift in 1925. The purple crepe was scraps from my mother's wedding dress that Grandma also made. I can't bear to part with that one. But we do have new quilts we sell for the ladies in our church. Let me show you a few," the red-cheeked shop owner offered, pushing her round spectacles higher on her nose.

"Yes, these are beautiful," I said. "But that Sunshine and Shadow took my breath away and now nothing else will do after seeing it." We thanked her for telling us about her Amish quilting traditions and for showing us the beautiful workmanship. Then we headed out to leave.

Though we left empty-handed, we almost filled the van as we opened the doors to get in. The blue van was totally covered with thousands of huge black horseflies stuck to every surface. We jumped in and started the windshield wipers, which cleared enough of a peephole to see through to drive. We took off, hoping the wind would blow the rest away. But no, they clung like glue until we'd reached speeds of sixty miles per hour before the last of the pesky bugs released their death grip. Seems they'd had their fill of the aromatic pig farm and latched on to our van as the means of escape.

We laughed 'til we cried all the way home. "Nobody will ever believe this story. We should've taken a picture of our great flies and entered it in the Guinness Book of Records," I told Linda. "I could write a book on the perils and adventures of a quilt dealer from Oklahoma."

*"The LORD is my shepherd; I shall not want. He makes me to lie down in green pastures; He leads me beside the still waters. He restores my soul;" Psalm 23-1-3a*

# Emmajean's Lifelong Passion

### by Judy Howard

Emmajean Lenard was born in a small white clapboard farmhouse outside Enid, Oklahoma in 1909, just two years after statehood. Her mother and grandmother lovingly taught her to quilt at an early age. By her late teens, Emmajean had filled her hope chest with a baker's dozen quilts.

Their family prospered on their homestead, despite the hardships of pioneer life, and Emmajean grew up to be a lovely young lady with many admirers. She met Earl Templeton at college. After a lengthy courtship, they married and moved to Kentucky, leaving the only home she'd ever known.

Earl moved quickly up the banking success ladder with the help of Emmajean's gracious social skills and hostessing abilities. Soon she was entertaining the elite bankers from around the state and nation as Earl was appointed to one state and national banking commission office after another.

Though she grieved not having children, Emmajean volunteered her time helping others and spent any idle time she had with needle and thread, pursuing her passion — quilting.

Emmajean and Earl spent vacations and winters in their second home in Florida. And while Earl pursued his passion of fishing, Emmajean entertained herself with appliquéing breathtaking quilt tops in patterns of rose, iris, gladiola, bridal wreath and poppy. When she returned to Kentucky each spring, she commissioned the mountain women in her area to hand-quilt the tops.

Though it seems tragic that Emmajean had no children to whom she could pass on the quilts, she folded them away and stored them unused by the dozens. The quilts brought great joy to Emmajean in their making and rave reviews at quilt shows and county fairs.

After the death of her beloved husband, Emmajean moved back home to Enid to be near her remaining family. She died in 2004 at the age of ninety-three, leaving a stash of the most glorious pristine quilts to her nieces and nephews, friends and neighbors—a legacy of her grace and beauty as evidenced by a lifetime poured into her quilts. I was fortunate to buy some of her heirlooms at her estate sale. Her Rose Nosegay Appliqué adorns the title and chapter pages of *Heavenly Patchwork I.*

> *"Let your conduct be without covetousness; be content with such things as you have. For He Himself has said, 'I will never leave you nor forsake you.' So we may boldly say: 'The LORD is my helper; I will not fear. What can man do to me?'" Hebrews 13:5-6*

# Zac Quilts Prize-Winner for Oklahoma State Fair

*as told by Jackie Smith to Judy Howard*

Zac, my best buddy and grandson, and I garden, travel, play ball and read together. And every Sunday before church, we make blueberry muffins. When Zac was six, we read a book about a boy and his grandmother's making a quilt together.

"Can we do that, Gramby?" Zac asked excitedly.

"But of course, sweetheart. Anything you'd like to do. You know I love to quilt. Would you like to help me pick out a pattern?"

"You bet. Can I paint sailboats, fire engines, trucks and doggies on it?"

"Sounds like a great idea. I have some muslin, stencils and acrylic paints we can use. It will be lots of fun."

After months of hard work—mostly mine—we completed our first quilt together. Zac was ecstatic. And I'll have to admit, the quilt was quite striking and received rave reviews from Zac's mom. "Why don't you enter it in the State Fair next month?" she suggested.

That's all Zac could talk about. When the fair finally opened, we raced down the aisles looking for our quilt. Zac ran ahead and immediately returned, beaming.

"We won, we won! Hurry, Gramby," he shouted, as he grabbed my hand and jumped up and down. "We won a ribbon."

My heart burst with pride as I soaked in Zac's bright smile and his joy, knowing he'd treasure the moment forever.

As we walked around, reveling in the win, Zac overheard two ladies discussing the quilts. "Would you like to see my quilt?" Zac asked these strangers. "I won a ribbon, too."

Zac's smile spread even wider as the women graciously praised his quilt. It was a cherished moment in both of our lives.

Proud Grandma then – even prouder Grandma now. Zac serves his country as a U.S. Marine in Iraq. He appears so stern and fierce in his official Marine photo, but I'll always remember that six year old with the big bright smile, strutting around in victory over his first quilt at the State Fair..

*"But thanks be to God, who gives us the victory through our Lord Jesus Christ. Therefore, my beloved brethren, be steadfast, immovable, always abounding in the work of the Lord, knowing that your labor is not in vain in the Lord." I Corinthians 15:57-58*

# The Apple Pie that Brought the House Down

*as told by Marilea Ryder to Judy Howard*

"I know this isn't as pretty as the Civil War quilt I gave you last Christmas," Bernice said as she handed her daughter Marilea Ryder a handmade blanket wrapped in tissue. But I knew you would appreciate it nonetheless."

"What's the story behind it?"

"I remember it as if it were yesterday even though I was a small child," Bernice began. "Aunt Clair was visiting our farm in Newark, Arkansas one September day and decided to help while we went to church by baking an apple pie from apples she'd just picked in our orchard. After peeling, coring, slicing, sweetening and dumping the apples into her prize-winning pie crust, she slid the pie into our old wood stove and went back outside to gather eggs.

When she opened the door of the cabin with her apron loaded with eggs, she smelled scorched apples and saw the potholder on top of the stove blazing and the curtains nearby catching fire. Left alone with no running water to drench the flames, Claire was powerless to quench the fire. The log cabin quickly burned to the ground before the family returned home from church.

Word quickly spread and church friends and neighbors came with a feast to share along with clothing and a few necessities. After dinner, the men began rebuilding the cabin while the women gathered their feedsacks and scraps and held a quilting bee to replace the warm bedding for the upcoming winter.

"Though this hand-tied comforter isn't beautiful like your Tulip Applique', it's precious to me. This quilt represents God's love in action as demonstrated by our caring friends and truly is a comforter in every sense," Bernice explained. "I hope you'll cherish it forever."

*"Therefore, to him who knows to do good and does not do it, to him it is sin."*
*James 4:17*

# Sacrificial Love

*as told by Zolalee Gaylor*
*to Judy Howard*

At age five, my first dramatic encounter with quilting was when Pricilla Peabody hired Mamma to quilt a Lone Star top for $5 in 1933. I remember Mama's fingers were always raw and bleeding, because Priscilla insisted on using a tightly woven percale for the backing, which was almost impossible to get a needle through.

"Mamma, why are you crying?" I remember asking her as she hung up the phone one day. Mama was also teaching me to quilt at the same time on my own Four Patch.

"Oh, Zolalee, don't be upset. Mommy's just tired, working day and night to finish this quilt on time. Priscilla keeps pushing me to hurry. She's such a perfectionist and doesn't understand how long it takes to make a quilt by hand."

Several months later, the Lone Star was completed. Priscilla immediately entered it in the state fair where it won a blue ribbon. She gave no credit to my mother. I felt sad for Mama and angry at this pushy lady.

Sixty years later while in Springfield, Missouri, giving a lecture to the quilt guild, I visited my youngest brother Niles. I shared this story with him about our mom who had worked so hard to provide for her three boys and one girl during the Depression when Dad was out of work for two years.

"Would you like to know how that hard-earned $5 was spent?" Niles asked, remembering something long forgotten. "That $5 bought our oldest brother a pair of tennis shoes so he could play basketball in high school."

Whenever I read Proverbs 31, I think of Mom, especially verse 28, "Her children rise up and call her blessed."

> *"Who can find a virtuous wife?*
> *For her worth is far above rubies...*
> *her lamp does not go out by night...*
> *Give her of the fruit of her hands,*
> *and let her own works praise her..."*
> *Proverbs 31:1,18b,31*

# *Ida's Legacy*
### by Judy Howard

"I've never seen such a beautiful collection of quilts, mostly in mint condition. Do you know their history?" I asked Bill Elam as he showed me the thirteen quilts he wanted to sell. Included were a Flower Garden, Snowball, Bowtie, Ocean Wave, Irish Chain and Dahlia, Crazy and others.

"But of course. Grandmother Ida Pierson Elam born in 1890 made these quilts on her farm in northwest Missouri before 1935. She was forced to work her farm alone in 1922 after she divorced," Bill said. To support her twelve-year-old son Gifford, Ida quilted for hire, drove the horse-drawn school wagon, and worked as a telephone operator, housekeeper and cafeteria worker at a nursing home.

"It sounds like Ida was a hard-working, strong woman to have survived the Depression without a spouse."

"That's not half her tragic story. This is a picture of Grandmother in 1912 when my dad was two. When he was twenty-seven, he died on his wife's twenty-first birthday when I was only three. Ida raised me and worked full-time despite her failing eyesight which didn't allow her to quilt after 1935," Bill continued.

"Do you think this 1800's Crazy quilt and red and green appliqué were made by Ida's mother?" I asked trying to further piece together the Elam's life history.

"Most assuredly. I remember Grandmother telling how her mother taught her to take tiny stitches when she was only four," Bill recalled. He pulled his Nine-Patch baby quilt from the stack, but confessed that he wasn't selling the exquisite appliquéd circus quilt she created for him, along with a couple of other special ones.

Since Bill didn't have children, he wanted to find a good home for Ida's quilts—someone who would appreciate their heritage. "After reading your *Heavenly Patchwork* book I thought you might be the perfect care-giver for my grandmother's quilts."

> *"My soul, wait silently for God alone,*
> *for my expectation is from Him.*
> *He only is my rock and my salvation;*
> *He is my defense; I shall not be moved."*
> *Psalm 62:5-6*

**21**

**2**

**18**

**21**

**22**

**18**

16

21

2

18

16

7

5

79

62

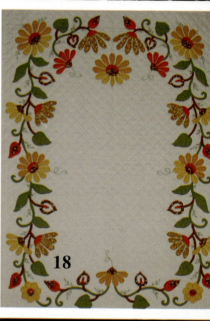

18

21

22

86

87

87

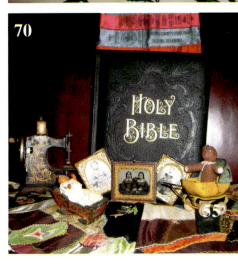

70

55

56

79

62

68

70

68

70

165

79

22

81

70

84

64

64

16

79

64

66

57

64

76

76

87

56

57

70

Oklahoma Diamond Jubilee Quilt

59

81

64

79

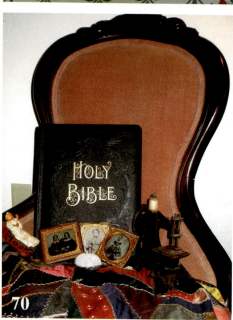

70

83

**64**

**62**

**79**

**87**

**64**

**56**

74

62

64

81

74

64

62

88

70

124

117

112

113

123

121

113

119

113

131

115

113

117

113

119

126

119

117

113

**173**

**94**

**132**

**167**

**14**

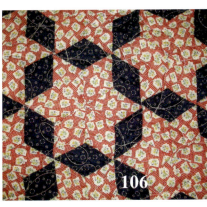

**106**

165

5

22

Oklahoma Quilt

132

175

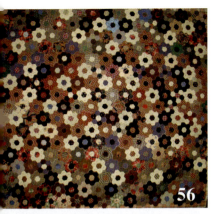

56

5

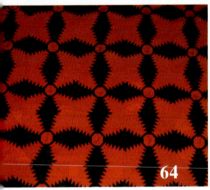

64

56

70

56

157

123

115

127

157

134

21

113

173

1908 SCHOOL 1936

130

104

131

106

117

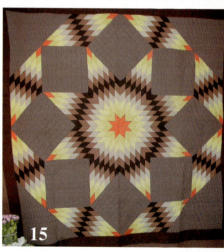

15

117

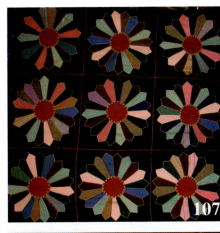

107

106

106

119

103

104

148

98

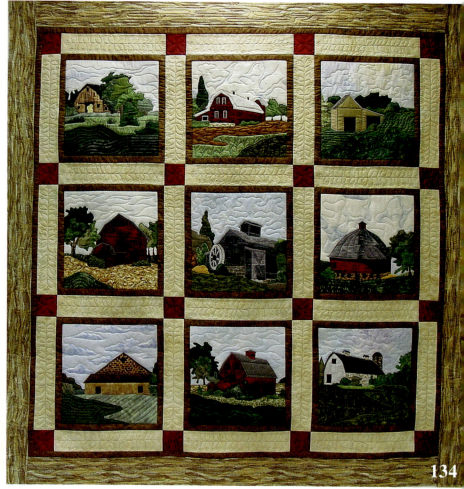

134

56

142

143

42

139

141

154

148

**154**

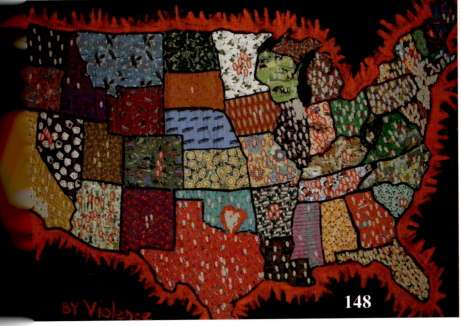

BY Violence

**148**

154

154

152

151

156

154

154

154

154

154

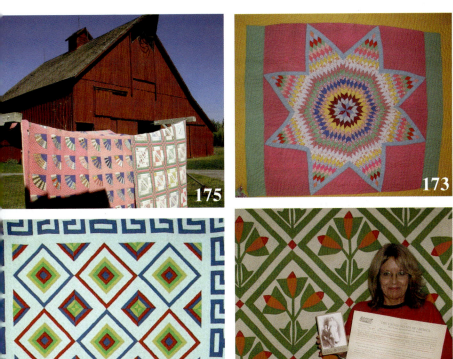

175

173

168

157

167

162

60

173

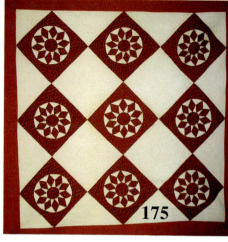

175

175

164

170

173

# Legacy Quilts

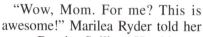

# Civil War Quilts Buried and Resurrected

*as told by Marilea Ryder
to Judy Howard*

"Wow, Mom. For me? This is awesome!" Marilea Ryder told her mom, Bernice Sullivan Hawkins, as Marilea excitedly unwrapped the Christmas present containing a red and green tulip appliqué. "Would you look at this fabulous hand-quilting in one inch circles all over the quilt. Was this your grandmother's quilt?"

"No, actually it was your great- great-grandmother Hattie's quilt from her plantation near Germantown, Tennessee. I wanted to keep it in the family and knew you would appreciate it," Bernice replied, delighted that her daughter was so thrilled. "Hattie supposedly used the end of a spool of thread for the quilting template. Can you imagine?"

Bernice went on to explain that during the Civil War when Sherman's troops were marching through the south burning and looting everything in sight, Hattie ordered the slaves to wrap the silver in this Tulip quilt and bury it, except for the coffee pot. There was hot coffee in the pot, so Hattie quickly dumped the coffee and hid the pot under her hoop skirt. Unfortunately Hattie jumped when one of the soldiers pinched her. Out tumbled the coffeepot which they confiscated along with everything else of value they could carry off. After the army passed through the area, the slaves dug up the silver and quilts.

"This Tulip quilt doesn't even look like it's been used—not to mention being buried and unearthed during the Civil War nearly 150 years ago," Marilea observed after examining it further. "What an amazing story of survival. I think I'll type the history onto muslin and sew it on the back for my grandchildren."

"What a great idea," Bernice said as she hugged Marilea. "I knew you would be the perfect custodian to preserve our family heritage and keepsake."

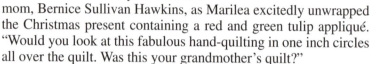

*"Jesus said to her, 'I am the resurrection and the life. He who believes in Me, though he may die, he shall live. And whoever lives and believes in Me shall never die. Do you believe this?'"*
*John 11:25*

# Sunset Carson Rides Again in Oklahoman's Memory

### as told by Thelma Powell
### to Judy Howard

Voted one of Hollywood's top ten cowboy stars, Sunset Kit Carson was born in 1920 in Gracemont, Oklahoma as Winifred Maurice Harrison when Thelma was only four. "We spent many happy childhood days hanging out together as cousins," Thelma said. Tall, dark and handsome Sunset Carson had rescued Thelma's dad Lee from drowning. The kinfolk were camping and fishing at Washita Lake. Lee got his boot tangled up in tree roots while he was seining beside the boat and went under the water, gasping three times. Winifred jumped in and effortlessly pulled Lee out of the lake and became Thelma's personal hero from that day forth.

Winifred always was a big show-off. "Why, I remember him trick riding on his horse, jumping from one side of the saddle to the other all the way from the barn to the gate," Thelma recalled. Winifred was a crack shot and impressed his cousins by shooting a piece of chalk from between their fingers with his .22 caliber rifle.

Sunset Carson always will be Oklahoma's cowboy hero, especially after making twenty-six movies and appearing in countless comic books and his Wild Wild West traveling shows on Cactus, his white horse.

Winifred's sister, along with other female cousins and friends, made quilt blocks and embroidered their names for Thelma's 1933 Friendship quilt made when she graduated from high school.

"What did you do for fun growing up on the farm?" I asked Thelma.

"I remember riding back from the fields straddling my sister's cotton sack when I was small, shouting 'Giddiup' all the way home. After milking the cows, gardening, sewing and completing the other farm chores, we'd walk to each other's farmhouses for a party, listening to those thick brown records on the graph phone," Thelma said.

Thelma's parents and the Spring Creek Baptist Church, which is still going strong, didn't condone dancing, so they didn't participate in the country hoedowns.

But each summer, the family loaded up in the wagon and headed to Binger for the Indian campgrounds. "While Mom and Dad were selling ice cream to the Indians, my sister and I snuck into line with the Indians for their stomp dancing with drums thundering in the middle," Thelma confessed. When they got too tired to keep up, they'd stretch out their quilt pallets on the ground to spend the night.

It was only one mile as the crow flies to the one-room Bald Knob Schoolhouse, so naturally they hiked through the fields in rain or snow. Thelma's mother made her daughters butterfly dresses which consisted of two pieces of calico joined together with the neck cut out. When the sisters raised their arms they looked like butterflies winging their way to school, each in a different color, decorating the countryside.

"Mom and Grandmother taught me how to quilt and sew our clothing and bonnets. Mostly we used feed sacks and dress scraps for the quilts. We grew and carded our own cotton for the bats," Thelma explained. With nine children, it took lots of sewing to keep the family clothed and warm. "My sister died of appendicitis when I was five. Mom and Dad rushed my sister to the nearest doctor in the wagon, but didn't make it in time.

"I'll never forget standing on top of the fat fence post in the front yard, straining to see the clouds of dust rise along the cottonwood tree-lined lane," Thelma said. It was a contest to see who could catch the first glimpse of sister Molly's beau coming to court her in his buggy. A few years later, Thelma's parents bought one of the first cars Ford rolled off its assembly line, so Thelma's courting days were much improved.

They never went hungry through the Depression, being self-sufficient with their granary, dairy cattle, orchards, vegetable garden and vineyard. "I met my husband Pheo Powell at the Baptist church in Anadarko where I was attending business college." After getting married, Thelma and Pheo moved to Hobart, Elk City, Carnegie and finally settled in Oklahoma City for the last fifty years.

"But those early childhood days in Caddo County spawned lots of fond memories," Thelma admitted wistfully. "I've written family histories, tape recorded tales of remembrance and compiled scrapbooks bulging with early Oklahoma farmstead photos for each of my children. Someday they'll appreciate having tangible records of their ancestors' heritage."

> *"Your name, O LORD, endures forever,*
> *Your fame, O LORD, throughout all generations."*
> *Psalm 135:13*

# Patches from the Past

*as told by Jeannette Gilliam*
*to Judy Howard*

It was a bitter, snowy New Year's Day ushering in 1916 on a farm outside Hiawatha, Kansas. Forty horses and buggies and a few Model Ts were parked outside the farmhouse. Inside, dozens of women cooked and served lunch to their families, neighbors, friends and their minister, who'd driven out in a hurry from town. Anyone passing by would have thought it was a grand New Year's Celebration.

It was a celebration of a different kind. A celebration of the life of Florence McCroy, the loving wife and mother of five children. Florence was a fine Bible scholar and Presbyterian Sunday school teacher, a real dynamo though she stood only five foot tall in her best Sunday heels.

The doctor had arrived before midnight, everyone thought so that he could usher in a new life—a New Year's baby. But there were complications, and both Florence and the baby began their new life in heaven, instead.

Six-year-old Jeannette, the youngest in the family, was devastated. "I want my mama!" she sobbed. "Who's going to take care of me?"

"We'll make it just fine with God's help," Papa replied, gathering Jeannette into his lap to console her. "Mary and Margaret can handle the cooking, cleaning and sewing. We'll just have to depend on God and each other more."

Little Jeannette was forced to grow up fast without a mother. Sisters Mary and Margaret tried hard to take their mother's place. They even sewed their baby sister's clothes in blue to match her expressive eyes. Jeannette was a good student and each year her teachers rewarded her for never missing a day of school despite having to walk, often through snow, one and a half miles each way to her one-room schoolhouse.

When Jeannette was fourteen, her father remarried, sold the five large farms the family had homesteaded and moved to town where he opened a cattle sales barn. Jeannette was forced to move in with her aunt, because her step-mother didn't want her. Again, she was devastated.

But Jeannette was a fighter and rose above her heartaches. She continued to excel in school, remained on the honor roll, served as president of the girl's club and even earned the lead part in the play *Babs*. She couldn't wait to get to school the day after the newspaper claimed she was the best lead actress in Hiawatha. Unfortunately, while hurrying there, she fell on the ice, fainted, and had to be carried home to her aunt's home where she was diagonosed with cerebral meningitis. The doctor said Jeannette would never survive, but she knew better and never doubted that God would heal her. She spent the next two months flat on her back and never completed high school.

When Jeannette fully recovered, she moved into her grandmother's boarding house where she was forced to work for her own room and board from dawn to dusk because they were so poor.

During WWII, Jeannette worked for J. S. Lerner's and later moved to Topeka, Kansas to work at the Santa Fe Railroad office earning $150 a month. While living in Topeka, Jeannette met Henry Gilliam at a dance. Henry wooed and courted her and within a year they married and moved to Oklahoma City.

In 1996, Jeannette came into my shop, Buckboard Antiques & Quilts. She brought along her prized Friendship quilt and asked me to appraise it.

"What do you know about the quilt?" I asked.

"It's dated 1845 and was probably made for Anna McCreight Culp's birth," Jeannette explained. It contained the names and Pennsylvania addresses, signed in ink, of the friends and relatives of Jeannette's great-grandmother Margaret Montgomery McCreight of Union City, Pennsylvania.

"Have you done any research to find out who these people were?" I asked.

"Why yes, I have the Daughters of the American Revolution papers tracing my ancestors back to Charles Dale, whom King William the Third sent with the troops from England to Ireland in 1590. Dale's ancestors came to America as Presbyterian missionaries in 1766, settling in Chester County, Pennsylvania."

Dale's youngest son Samuel was a member of the first organized House of Assembly and a 1795 Senator of Pennsylvania, after serving as Captain in the Revolutionary War. On the other side of the family, Captain Thomas Strawbridge, father-in-law of General Daniel Montgomery, became a member of the First Constitutional Convention. His grandson served as medical director on the staff of General Curtis and the grandson was elected to Congress.

"This quilt belongs in a museum in Pennsylvania or in the

Smithsonian," I suggested. "It's a fabulous link to early American history."

"But it's the only tie I have left to my family," objected Jeannette. "I'm the only survivor who remembers my grandfather who came from Pennsylvania to Hiawatha. My family was well-educated and well-bred. The women were accomplished needle workers who created beautiful clothing, linens, lace and quilts. My mama had many quilting parties and she made a beautiful Rose of Sharon appliquéd quilt for my sister's hope chest."

She began to fold up her treasure to take home. "I couldn't possibly part with the family memories. This quilt is the only tangible item I have that tells the story of my family roots."

That's when Jeannette began to tell me her story. "Since I lost my mother when I was only six, and my father basically deserted me when I was fourteen, this family Album quilt gives me my identity and heritage. Each time I read those names, I remember these peoples' faces from Mother's scrapbook. And I relive the tales she told me of their part in settling America, fighting the Indians and Britons for our nation's freedom. And I feel good that some of my family had a role in writing our Constitution." She looked melancholy, but firm in her decision. "Maybe I'll donate it to the Smithsonian at my death. They can preserve it and go on sharing my family's story of founding America with school children for generations to come." With that, Jeannette gathered her "family" around her to take back to comfort her during her living years in her home in Oklahoma City.

*"Indeed, my heritage is beautiful to me. I have set the LORD always before me. Because he is at my right hand, I will not be shaken."*
*Psalm 16:6b, 8 NIV*

## Poor Yet Rich in Spirit

*as told by Marilea Ryder to Judy Howard*

Seventy-nine-year-old Nita McKnight has discovered the secret to true happiness. Living on $4,800 per year, Nita used what little money she could scrape together to buy materials to complete twenty-five small hand-made quilts this year to give unwed mothers, the homeless, and those less fortunate than she is. She exemplifies a generous heart of sacrificial love.

*". . . this poor widow has put in more than all those who have given to the treasury, for they all put in out of their abundance, but she out of her poverty put in all that she had, her whole livelihood." Mark 12:43-44*

# Indian Moccasins for Quilts

*as told by Bessie Elston*

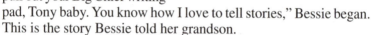

"MeMaw, what was it like when you were a child?" ten-year-old Anthony Riggs asked his great-grandmother Bessie Elston over the phone. "We're studying Oklahoma history in school and I need to write a paper."

"Sharpen your pencil and pull out your Big Chief writing pad, Tony baby. You know how I love to tell stories," Bessie began. This is the story Bessie told her grandson.

We moved around a lot when I was little. My dad Bill Huckins worked at a grain elevator and as a butcher in Thomas, Oklahoma, and later owned Bill's IGA. His cousin owned the historic Huckins Hotel in Oklahoma City.

My granddad Sherman Huckins lived in Kansas and worked on the railroad until he bought a farm near Beaver, Oklahoma where I was born in 1922. To supplement his meager income, my dad worked for WPA (Works Progress Administration), building Highway 270. Because my grandparents' farm couldn't support two families through The Great Depression and Dust Bowl Days, my parents left their family farm in 1934.

Dad played the banjo, Mom played the piano, and my brother played guitar for entertainment. Bluegrass music was our family's first love. My fondest memories are of the community dances and potluck feasts at neighboring farm houses. After working hard in the fields all week, everyone was ready to celebrate big time. And of course we went to lots of country rodeos. I remember helping Mom make quilts and learning how to sew dresses when I was twelve. We had lots of fun at the quilting bees.

Mom must have grown up deprived of bed covers, because she pieced together every scrap of fabric she could lay her hands on. She made hundreds of quilts to keep us warm. I've still got twenty-five of her quilts. Mom gave them away to anyone in need, including Eva Ocrow, her good Indian friend and neighbor in Thomas. Eva often watched TV at our house as she beaded Indian moccasins for my dolls. I went to school with Eva's son along with Mary Whitetail, Gertrude Longbear and Nettie Drunkard. Amish and Mennonite children also attended our school. We were always amazed to see their scraggly-bearded fathers dressed in buttoned-front black pants "carpool" them to school in horse-drawn buggies.

Most of the Indian kids lived in government-built bungalows. In the summertime, they lived in hogans built from tree limbs and teepees. I lay awake and listened to them beating their drums all night in the summertime during their stomp dancing. Once I went to the bizarre funeral of an Indian friend who was killed in WWII. For the funeral, the Indians wore their quill and beaded leather clothing, moccasins, trade blankets and feather headdresses. The ceremonial dancing, drumming, chanting, feasting and pipe-smoking lasted the weekend long.

When I was nineteen, Lloyd and I met in Beaver at my aunt's farm. We fell madly in love and married two months later because it was too far to drive to date. Here we are still married sixty-three years later. We started married life on a farm in Forgan where your great-granddaddy Lloyd worked. Then we moved every year from one farm job to the next. At the last farm, Lloyd harvested and cured sweet potatoes.

Finally in 1943, Lloyd got a job for six straight years driving a delivery route for Coca Cola in Perryton, Texas. Mom even made a quilt from his salmon and green pin-striped Coke uniforms.

We finally put down roots in 1970 in Woodward, Oklahoma where we opened up Lloyd's Trading Post, which we ran until 1983. Since I've spent a lifetime sewing clothes for others, it seemed natural to start custom-making leather chaps for the rodeo riders and workers while Lloyd repaired their boots, saddles and harnesses. Your great-granddad even rode cutting horses in their rodeo.

In the 1980s after we got saved at an old-fashioned tent revival, we joined the cowboys at Cowboy Church on Thursday nights at the Beaver Baptist Church. I sang in the choir, taught Sunday school and helped in the kitchen cooking meals for funerals and church events.

Your baby quilt was Mama's last quilt made when she was eighty-seven. I don't know how she had the patience to sew those postage stamp size pieces together by hand. She must have been trying to use up her scraps that spanned five generations before she died.

*"The memory of the righteous is blessed, but the name of the wicked will rot." Proverbs 10:7*

## Twentieth Century Time Capsule

*as told by John and Bambi McBride*

"Going once . . . going twice," the balding auctioneer announced, folding up the century-old quilt. "Sold to John McBride and his bride Bambi, antique dealers from Winfield, Kansas."

After the auction, an elderly, distinguished-looking gentleman approached the McBrides, asking if they'd be interested in buying the remainder of his aunt's possessions. "She's 105 years old and I can't hold an estate sale in Aunt Marie's house, because she'd raise Cain if she ever found out." After Marie had lived her life in the house that her grandparents built one hundred years ago, her nephew finally persuaded her to move to Iowa to live with him.

"Oh, believe me, we understand how independent she is," Bambi said. "Our daughter took piano lessons from Marie ten years ago."

Several weeks later after buying the contents of Marie's home, John and Bambi explored the three-storey brick house. Searching through the full basement, stacked floor to ceiling with boxes containing magazines, newspapers and mail labeled neatly in chronological order 1920 through 1980, the experienced dealers were puzzled to discover piles of sacks overflowing in disarray around the foot of the stairway. "These bags must contain the last fifteen years' collection of papers Marie dropped from the head of the stairs when she no longer could climb the stairs," Bambi surmised. "Let's check out the attic and upstairs bedrooms. I'll bet nobody's been in those rooms in decades."

Bambi's instincts were correct. Deep dust showed that nothing had been disturbed in ages. One bedroom contained priceless handmade linens and lace from the early 1900's. From other family documents, photos, postcards and letters, Bambi and John pieced together Marie's fascinating story, including her three steamship trips to Europe in 1928, 1929 and 1930. They learned that Marie's grandfather Lt. Colonel Francis Hills commanded the 45th Pennsylvania Voluntary Infantry in the Fredericksburg confrontation during the Civil War, and he was one of the seven brothers founding Hills Brothers Coffee Company.

From the letters and bank records, the McBrides discovered that life-long spinster Marie barely had supported herself the last seventy years. She taught piano but only charged $3-$6 for lessons. Marie's twin sister moved to Ft. Worth to teach in the Wesleyan Women's College, leaving Marie alone those years after Marie cared for her parents until their deaths.

Carefully prying open an old camel back trunk, Bambi shouted, "John. Come look at these great old quilts. They've never seen the light of day." Gently unfolding the first of many, Bambi admired the beautiful double rose and white Flying Geese quilt, hand-pieced entirely in one-inch triangles. "Judging from the calico, I'll bet Daisy, Marie's mom, made this one before Marie was born." Bambi and John already had determined that Marie's dad was a dignitary and real estate mogul. It was a short jump to assume Daisy must have been a society lady with household help to afford her the luxury of time for such fine needlework.

"If quilts could only talk, we could step back in time into the lives of Marie's family," Bambi concluded, awestruck. "Then we'd be able to experience this family's joys, sorrows, heartaches and victories documented in each stitch. I could write a book with the priceless history in Marie's life-long time capsule."

## Nothing New Under the Sun
### by Judy Howard

Eight feet above our patio door in the living room hangs a striking red and green Rose Wreath appliquéd quilt, measuring three by twelve feet. I rarely look up to drink in its beauty. Only when visitors exclaim and ask its history do I stop to reconsider it.

"Oh, that's my Civil War quilt made by a widow in mourning," I tell friends. This young widow's husband had doctored the wounded soldiers on the battlefields then tragically died in action himself.

"But why's it so long and skinny?" everyone asks next.

So I explain how this long ago quilt was constructed by the block, just like our modern techniques. Though the appliqué is by hand, the quilting was exquisitely done on one of the first treadle sewing machines, a status symbol of that time. This widow used a half-inch crosshatch pattern.

In order to hang this beautiful work of art above my door in this long narrow space, I merely removed the basting threads connecting the blocks and borders and sewed them together end to end. "It just goes to prove that there's nothing new under the sun." *Ecc. 1:9*

*"They shall fear You as long as the sun and moon endure, throughout all generations.". Psalm 72:5*

# *Threads*

## by Mary Jewett

Grandma's sewing machine was the old-fashioned pedal variety, well-used and carefully tended. Colorful calicos and ginghams cut into tiny squares and triangles littered her worktable. Spools of thread lined the windowsill. Grandmother made quilts – Bowties, Spinning Bobbins, and sometimes the more difficult Double Wedding Ring.

As a child, I stood beside my grandmother, arranging the pieces and discussing the color combinations and patterns. I'd hand her each piece as she worked, her foot pumping the sewing machine pedal. As the blocks emerged from the sewing machine, I pressed them flat, trimmed the threads, and stacked the pretty new designs neatly on the table. Our heads bent close, our voices low, Grandma and I discussed many things as we worked. And Grandma told me stories, such as this:

"This is the pattern I used for the county fair in 1924 when the judges awarded me first place. I don't think Mrs. Morris ever forgave me for breaking her winning streak. Forty years and she still avoids me in the grocery," Grandma tsked and shook her head.

When each quilt was finished, Grandmother stitched the date onto a corner of the blanket. "These old eyes," she'd sigh, handing me the needle to thread for her. Once the needle was threaded, I'd watch as Grandma pulled it in and out, the thimble sparkling on her finger. Those simple letters and numbers felt like Braille against the soft fabric.

Then, with a flip of her wrists, Grandma snapped the quilt into the air. We'd watch it float for a moment before settling across the table where we smoothed it flat with the palms of our hands. This was always our first look at the completed project – our first look at the repeating pattern of the fabrics and colors creating the blocks.

Grandma marked the major events and milestones in my life with the gift of a quilt. On the first day of kindergarten, I received the Schoolhouse pattern – the schoolhouses worked in bright red calico against a brilliant white background. On my sweet sixteenth birthday, Grandmother surprised me with the Flower Basket pattern in blues and yellows. And for my wedding, she gave me with a lovely Double Wedding Ring quilt in a variety of pastels. Always, she kept these projects hidden from me – working only when I was not around. She took pleasure in my surprise.

The patterns of the blankets mirrored the patterns of my life. Each new quilt was a new set of stories. The things Grandmother and I had discussed over the hum of the sewing machine— her memories from the past and my dreams for the future— were as connected to the quilt as if they were written on the blocks.

"Remember this?" Grandmother would ask. "This piece is from the dress you wore on your first day of school. And this," she'd say, reaching for another square, "is from your great-grandmother's apron. I found it stored in the old trunk." Even if the moths got at it, Grandmother managed to salvage a few good scraps. No scrap of fabric was ever wasted. Grandmother's holding onto a dress or apron would have been a waste of material, while a quilt became a sentimental reminder of important events.

Grandmother is gone now. While I miss her no less as the years pass, each time I wrap myself in her quilt, I feel her presence. She gave me a gift by entrusting me with the stories of her life which I'm sharing with the next generation– retelling her tales of joy and hardship, love and laughter. By listening to my dreams, Grandmother also glimpsed my future – a future she would not be a part of . . . at least not in the physical sense.

But she always will be with me. Our lives are as interwoven as the blankets the two of us created. We are bound together by similar threads.

*"The works of the LORD are great . . .*
*He has made His wonderful works to be remembered;*
*the LORD is gracious and full of compassion."*
*Psalm 111:2a,4*

## The Wild West Indian Territory

*as told by Judy Qurazzo*
*to Judy Howard*

"I've slept under quilts since I was born," Judy shared with me when she sold me her beautiful red and green appliquéd Rose of Sharon quilt. "This was made by my great- great-grandmother Abigail McAdams in the mid-1800s in Bodarc, Missouri, population twenty-five. Abigail was an accomplished seamstress and also made intricately tucked christening gowns, white eyelet pantaloons, nightgowns and dresses."

Judy was full of fun stories from the past. She told me how Abigail loved her two huge hound dogs named Mutt and Jeff who were scared of lightning, thunderstorms and any body of water. Every time it stormed, the dogs tore through the screen door to get inside and hide under the table. To get Mutt and Jeff to come out again, Abigail merely threatened to throw a dipper of water on them and her mighty watch dogs meekly sulked out to lie near the potbellied stove again.

Abigail's daughter Elizabeth married Pierson Allen who, unfortunately, liked his beer. After returning from town on his horse, Pierson got drunker than a skunk and beat Elizabeth. Elizabeth threatened him, "If you ever get drunk again, I'm going to sew you up in a sheet and beat you with a buggy whip." Pierson did . . . and Elizabeth made good on her promise. Pierson never touched beer again.

Abigail had come from County Court, Ireland to South Bend, Indiana, before moving to Bodarc. In 1869, when Abigail's grandson John Joseph was seven, John traveled with his parents in a covered wagon to Indian Territory outside what is now Wann, Oklahoma. When John married in 1884, he moved his bride Lettie Jane to four sections of land near Copan, Oklahoma.

"John Joseph made the Oklahoma land run to obtain more land in 1889 and staked his claim on what is now downtown Stillwater,"

Judy remembered. She went on to say how three men stole his deed at gunpoint—the law of the land.

Later, John Joseph was the first to use artificial insemination in cattle. He also helped established the first Indian school. "That farm at Copan remained in the family passed down to my youngest uncle until that uncle died in 1988 and willed it to his friend," Judy said.

Judy's granddad drove the first heated school hay wagon. Early each morning, he heated rocks and placed them in the hay beneath where the children soon would huddle. "Because the Seminole Indian men thought my mom Sarah Ann was pretty, they teased her unmercifully at school and chased her on their paint ponies all the way home," Judy recalled. John Joseph remedied that by giving Sarah Ann a beautiful race horse to ride the one and a half miles to school. He advised her, "Give your horse the head, but hold on for dear life." Sarah Ann easily outran the paint ponies. When she arrived at the farm gate, her father was waiting with a shotgun. The Indians never bothered Sarah Ann again.

Sarah Ann was born in 1903, one of fifteen kids. She vowed to bear only two children after suffering the hardships of a large family on the frontier. Judy was born in 1942 in Bartlesville. Two months later, when WW11 began, Judy's dad Jessie Columbus Merideth was drafted to work at Tinker Air Force Base. He sold his fender and radiator shop next to the railroad tract and moved the family to Oklahoma City. Judy has lived in the same house for almost seventy years surrounded by her family quilts and memorabilia.

"It breaks my heart to sell my family heirlooms and these beautiful handmade quilts and needlework," Judy lamented.

"But I'm alone now and nearly blind. I'm forced to sell my home." She did feel good though about the legacy of her family's love and Oklahoma pioneer heritage living on in the stories and memories.

"Because Your lovingkindness is better than life,
my lips shall praise You . . .
My soul shall be satisfied . . . "
Psalm 63:3,5a

# *Oklahoma History Revealed in Quilts*

*by Judy Howard*

On a beautiful spring morning in March of 2005, I strolled through the booths at the Buchanan Antique Market in Oklahoma City, until a bright pumpkin and white quilt caught my eye. The one-inch sawtooth edges surrounding the central square within a square within another square, and within yet another square pattern made a stunning graphic work of art. And the quilting was superb in crosshatch, fleur de lis and floral quilting.

"What do you know about this quilt?" I asked the kind gentleman who helped me spread it out to further examine the fine workmanship.

"It was from my mom Wanda Koester's estate. She died in 1993 at the age of ninety-one. Her mother Clina Mueller, who immigrated to Ellis Island with her family from The Ukraine in Russia in 1892, made this quilt," Herschel Koester related as he introduced himself. "They settled in Minnesota. Wanda's father robbed a bank and came to Oklahoma to buy three farms—one for each of his children, if rumor can be believed. Our family still owns one of the original farms near Bessie, Oklahoma." Herschel shuffled around in some of his papers. "Here's the Land Grant Homestead Certificate signed by T. Roosevelt in 1901."

"What happened to the other two farms?" I asked, impressed that he knew so much interesting family history.

"Two of the sons mortgaged their farms to buy farm equipment and both went bankrupt in 1929. They fled with the thousands of other Okies in the *Grapes of Wrath* to California. Only because my mom and dad still farmed with a horse and plow were they able to survive the Great Depression and Dust Bowl Days."

"They must have had a strong faith in God to remain on the farm through those tough times," I said.

"Yes," he agreed. "They were devout Lutherans. In fact, their old church still stands in the middle of a wheat field, even though the farm buildings were destroyed by tornadoes in the 1960s." Herschel explained that the church celebrated its centennial in 1989 and told me how the farmers around Bessie spoke Volga German and helped each other through those disastrous times.

"Farming was not only financially risky, but also a dangerous occupation. In 1937 a horse kicked my granddad in the chest. Thinking nothing about it, he went back to the farmhouse and ate lunch," Herschel said. "He lay down for a little siesta and died in his sleep, leaving an even greater burden for the family to overcome. He was only forty-three years old. Only by total dependence on God did they persevere.

"Do you remember watching your mom quilt?" I asked.

"No, I don't think she had time with the farm chores. But her widowed mom lived with her family and must have been the quilter. I know they grew their own cotton and probably carded it for the cotton bats," Herschel continued. "Here's another quilt my grandmother made." He pulled out a beautiful hand appliquéd Flower Basket quilt. It was quilted with nine to eleven stitches per inch in one-half inch cross hatch and floral quilting all over it. "It's my favorite."

"I certainly can see why. It's absolutely exquisite!" I told him. "I'll bet it won the blue ribbons in every county and state fair. I've got to add these quilts to my collection," I said as I pulled out my checkbook. "Do you have any other information about the family or the quilts?"

"Oh sure, I have lots of pictures of my folks and of their farm in the early 1900s. I'll do a little digging and email them to you."

Meeting Herschel certainly made my day. His family history felt close enough to be my own and really made the quilts come alive to me.

If only quilts could talk—what stories they would tell... of hardships, sufferings, victories and joys and of a faithful Father who sustains and strengthens his people through them.

*"Through the LORD'S mercies we are not consumed,*
*because His compassions fail not.*
*They are new every morning; Great is Your faithfulness.*
*'The LORD is my portion,' says my soul, 'Therefore I hope in Him!'"*
*Lamentations 3:22-24*

# Every
## Remembrance of You
### *by Kay White Bishop*

"You want these old crazy quilts, Kay?" Aunt Kat asked as she prepared to move from her home of fifty years. "I've had them since I moved here to Bethany." Down they tumbled from the closet's top shelf with one yank.

"Are you *sure* no one else wants these?" I asked as I caught them.

"I want *you* to have them." Great Aunt Kathryn McLaughlin Shirey liked it when I went along with her ideas, but she still wished I'd wear socks and an undershirt during winter.

"This quilt is your great-grandmother's dresses, and the other is from my dad's suits. He died in '33."

I unfolded the heavy fabric to see rich random patchwork pieces of well-worn brown corduroy, soft black and white tweeds, and red woolen plaid. I buried my nose as if I could smell my great-grandfather James Longstreet McLaughlin's pipe tobacco.

"My dad came from West Virginia in 1910. He purchased 447 acres in Okay community. A year later, when I was two, Mama sold our house, and we girls took the train to Shawnee, finally arriving in Okay in a horse-drawn wagon."

"A wagon?" I said.

"My daddy raised horses and pigs. He hired the neighbors—Branson, Deatherage, Vandiver, Rider, Wade, and others—to work the cotton, corn, and hay fields. One night when I was real little, a loud noise shook me out of bed. Lightning hit the barn. Dad ran out into that fire-filled sky and tried to get the barn open, but it was too late."

"No!"

"I cried, but Mama cheered us up with her apple butter, popcorn, and Amos 'n Andy on the radio. We knitted and quilted all winter."

And now in my lap lay Great Grandmother Virginia Margaret Galford McLaughlin's weightless Crazy quilt unfurling a flower garden of pink carnations, white daisies and green leaves accented by vibrant polka dots in primary colors. My fingers outlined each angular piece joined to the next with meticulous embroidery stitches still intact.

"This quilt backing was Mama's old drapes," Aunt Kat explained. "I want you to have this wool coverlet, too. We raised the sheep, and Mama taught her Sunday school class to card and spin this very wool on her spinning wheel."

"Thanks," I said. She had given me so much of herself through the years that these antique pieces were the icing on the cake. My great-grandmother had died in 1954 when I was only six.

"Mama organized the community of Pink as she rode sidesaddle from house to house. She was a midwife, too. After our one-room school opened, she went door to door asking, 'Methodist, Presbyterian, or Baptist?' Up went the Baptist church. Brown Cemetery still holds the Claxtons and Stapps who married each other. We had such fun baking pies and sewing."

Aunt Kat's quilt frame revealed the yearly history of our relatives' marriages, births, and graduations. No fabric ever escaped the quilt. If she ran out of old clothing pieces, she shopped garage sales and TG&Y bargain tables. She later boosted our confidence and competency, teaching us crochet, knitting, and ceramics.

Her quilting, as well as wedding and prom dresses, provided continual loving conversation and celebration for the many material girls who knew Aunt Kat as Mimi, Aunt Kathryn, or Mrs. Shirey. She also tailored attention toward her nieces and nephews as every one of her seven siblings passed on before her. She continually adjusted to an ever-changing medium: homespun, feed sack, muslin, printed cotton, satin, and the double-knit polyester revolution of the 1970's.

"I can't tell your stitches from mine any more," she said to me one day as we finished my son Nick's baby quilt. *What a compliment!* But I feared it revealed more about her rapidly failing vision.

Aunt Kat left for Heaven January 19, 2005 at age ninety-five. I think of her often because her father's quilt tells its story on my entry hall bench, and her mother's flowery handiwork drapes beautifully from the back of my sofa. And the little plaque I gave her still boasts:

> *"I thank my God upon every remembrance of you."*
> *Philippians 1:3*

## Champion Blue Ribbon Winner

*as told by Ethel Howery to Judy Howard*

"Oklahoma history? Land yes!" ninety-six-year-old Ethel Howery told me when I asked her about sharing stories to celebrate Oklahoma's Centennial. "My grandparents wrote Oklahoma and Cleveland County history."

The Prices, Ethel's mother's parents, came in a covered wagon and homesteaded the site of the present Oklahoma City Downtown Airpark in the Land Run of 1889. "My father-to-be John A. Rath built a home for the Prices," Ethel explained. "Grandpa Teel and Grandpa Howery homesteaded in Cleveland County. Their sod dugouts were located near the intersection of 48th Avenue, S.E. and Cedar Lane Road in Norman."

Ethel's granddad died shortly after staking their claim and after the eighth child was born to their family. "To maintain our homestead," Ethel told me, "Mother, the oldest of the kids, had to clear three acres of land each year." This was particularly difficult in the river bottom, an area which was solid trees. "She was tough, though." Ethel laughed. "Just to prove how hardy she was, one time each winter Mom ran around the house three times barefoot. She lived to be ninety-nine.

"My paternal grandfather-in-law Richard Teel traded two mules for his homestead across from the Howery homestead," Ethel said. They had no doctors or grocery stores back then. Kids were more plentiful than cloth. So cloth was held in higher esteem. Their family saved every scrap to make quilts to keep warm in those drafty sod and clapboard houses.

"My mom and grandma taught me to quilt when I was five," Ethel said, remembering coming straight home from school when she was seven to finish her first quilt. She insisted on picking out her own store-bought calicos, much to her mother's disdain. Ethel wanted no part of those ugly haphazard scrapbag quilts everyone else made. Ethel sorted through their patterns before she found the one she wanted to use. "Everyone fussed that I was already a perfectionist at age seven." That was the beginning of Ethel's passion with quilt-making.

"How many do you suppose you've made?" I asked.

"Lands almighty, who could count," Ethel said. "I gave them away as fast as I made them. The strangest quilt I ever made was from green felt cloth stripped off a pool table," she said.

In 1936, Ethel helped found the Cleveland County Fair and each succeeding year she entered quilts, canning, and needlework in the competition.

"I bet that each year you came home with blue ribbons, didn't you?"

"Well, as a matter of fact, my son just counted up 787 ribbons, and more than half were blue." Ethel chuckled modestly.

I'd say her perfectionism paid off.

"What were your favorite patterns?" I wanted to know.

"Mom taught me to love Lone Stars and I made lots of Trips Around the World."

It was always a challenge for Ethel to plan the color schemes and buy just the perfect fabric to make each quilt pretty.

"I helped found the Home Demonstration Clubs and loved the fellowship of quilting with others," she told me, wistfully. "We met every week over lunch in each other's homes and had the best time."

"But what still drives you to spend thousands of hours creating your masterpieces?"

"Quilting was an excuse to get my friends together. We laughed, cried, grieved our losses and raised our children together. We shared our joys and triumphs and learned from each other." Ethel thought a minute, then explained, "The act of creating something beautiful was a gift I think I gave myself. And it was a rewarding way of showing my family how much I loved them by leaving a tangible legacy for each of them so I wouldn't be forgotten when I'm gone."

*" But the LORD*
*shall endure forever;"*
*Psalm9:7a*

# Dust Bowl Depression Days on the Farm

*as told by Harry Schoenhals to Judy Howard*

Born in 1931, Harry Schoenhals and his eight brothers and one sister were raised in a four-room unheated farmhouse in the Panhandle where the "northerlies" still blast through the flat wheat fields with a vengeance. During more than a few winter nights, temperatures dropped to 20° below. "That's when you wear every stitch of clothing you own and jump in bed between two goose feather mattresses with Mama's handmade comforters piled high to keep you warm," Harry recalled.

Harry helped his mom hold live geese upside down and pluck their feathers to stuff those warm mattresses and a few quilts, too. The whole family got involved tying the heavy patchwork comforters after their mom patched their old work clothes together to make the top. "They weren't pretty—but they sure were warm," Harry explained. As quilts wore out, Harry's mom used the tattered and torn quilts as stuffing for the next tops and backings she made. The worn-out comforters were never thrown away, but recycled to new life as window or door coverings to keep the drafts out in the winter or they were used as picnic blankets.

Thrift was a gene bred deep through the Schoenhals. Volga German was spoken in their home until Harry went to first grade. In the late 1600s when Queen Catherine II opened up Russia to German farmers, the Schoenhals were the first to go there. They were also some of the first to flee Russia with their neighbors in the 1890s to begin a new life of freedom in America when the Imperial Russian Government repealed their special privileges.

These German Russians became an important part of Oklahoma's history as they claimed free farm land and formed their German colonies and Congregational Churches, conducting worship in German until the late 1940s. Harry's dad was born in 1900 in Shattuck, Oklahoma. Harry's grandfather's three-storey homestead still stands—a testament to the fruit of their hard labor and work ethic.

"One summer Sunday, our family was visiting my aunt and uncle and picnicking down at the creek when Dad spotted a black cloud.

He grabbed the picnic basket and quilt and commanded us to jump in the car so we could race home before the dust storm hit." The family ran into the house just as the sky turned black. Frantically, the children prayed that their dad would make it back from the garage where he was parking the Model A. After thirty minutes when they had given up hope of ever seeing him again, he burst through the door saying, "I wrestled the wind and dust back to the farmhouse with one hand anchoring the quilt over my head so I could breathe and my other hand clinging to the fence to find my way. I thought I'd never make it."

The next morning, the Schoenhals inspected the damage and were distraught to discover that every plant in their garden and fields had been uprooted and was nowhere to be seen. Top soil and tumbleweeds, blown all the way down from Kansas, were piled six feet high against every cross fence in their path. The church called for a prayer meeting to ask God to provide for their farming community until they could replant the following spring—and God proved faithful once again.

Harry helped hand-milk twenty cows, tend the vegetable garden, fruit orchard, pigs and chickens. The family even raised guineas to sound the alarm for coyotes in the chicken coop. Harry was his dad's right hand machinery mechanic and helped plant and harvest wheat, maize, grapes, cherries and apricots. He also slaughtered and prepared  cows and pigs for eating. He separated cream and churned the butter. Being German, the Schoenhals always had a good supply of homemade sausage, weinerscnitzel, and pickles.

Fondly, Harry remembers his mom's fixing the best fried chicken for Sunday dinner's treat. Their social life revolved around church activities with quilting bees, watermelon feasts, covered dish suppers, ice cream socials, and barn raisings. What they needed in the way of seed or other necessities that they couldn't grow on the farm, they traded for in town with their eggs and cream.

In the late 1940's, the Schoenhals built a new house with a coal-fired potbelly stove in the kitchen-dining room, a parlor for Sunday visitors and a guest bedroom that was seldom used. Harry chuckled as he recalled a visiting couple who received the shock of their life when they fell through the new bed all the way to the floor and woke up the whole house. One of Harry's mischievous brothers had removed the bed slats before the guests arrived. His parents never figured out which boy it was and his siblings wouldn't divulge the secret. Harry remembers his mom and dad's moving lots of fifty-pound and one hundred-pound feed sacks to get the right calico fabrics to make the quilt that covered that guest bed.

Asked if he ever felt deprived growing up, Harry quickly replied, "Absolutely not! Though we had no money, we were rich in God's blessings and never went hungry, nor did we get into trouble for lack of something to keep us busy. Money couldn't buy the hands-on education I got on the farm. The hard times bonded us tightly in love as a family and a community. Even today, our family and church celebrate monthly with reunions. We were forced to depend on God and each other to survive. We always felt most blessed and were very grateful for His faithfulness to provide."

*"I will sing of the mercies of the LORD forever; with my mouth will I make known Your faithfulness to all generations." Psalm 89:1*

## God's Wake-up Call

*as told by Marilea Ryder*

"A truck driver—you've got to be kidding," I exclaimed as 100- pound Suzanne Wichtendahl told me about her past.

"When my children were small, my first husband left me for a truck-stop waitress," Suzanne said. "I had been working in dispatching for Freymiller Trucking, but switched to driving trucks to support my family."

Then in 2000, Suzanne had a brain aneurism and wasn't expected to live. "God hit me on the head with a frying pan," she says. That's when she learned to value each day as a precious gift from God.

Despite being diagnosed with a slow form of Lou Gehrigs Disease in 2003, Suzanne says that her last five years have been her best five years.

Suzanne and I met at Church of Good Shepherd in Yukon, Oklahoma and found we had a common bond through quilting. Despite increasing paralysis of both legs and arms, Suzanne has made more than sixty quilts for family and friends. She's generous with her time and resources through her card and phone encouragement ministries. Suzanne inspires me to reevaluate my priorities and live a thankful life in service to others, as if today were my last day on this earth.

*"Teach us to number our days and recognize how few they are; help us to spend them as we should."*
*Psalm 90:12 The Living Bible*

# The Saga of the Wagon Wheel Quilt Blocks

*by Wanda Branson*

In 1889, my grandparents Irene Jane and Frank Sade along with their four children traveled from Iowa in a covered wagon to homestead a farm north of present day Crescent, Oklahoma. Included in the wagon was Irene Jane's prized collection of quilt block patterns she had appliquéd onto a bed sheet.

Fording a river on their dangerous journey, everything in the wagon got soaked. Arriving safely on the other side, Grandmother spread out the wagon's soggy contents on the ground to dry. Not wanting to get her cherished quilt blocks dirty, she hung them over a wagon wheel. Unfortunately, the iron wagon wheel rim rusted some of the blocks and the sheet.

The Sades' first home was a sod dugout as they struggled to survive and tame their wilderness frontier. Later, they built a tiny log cabin to better weather the harsh dust storms and winters. Many years later, they settled into a frame house and Irene Jane turned her attention to quilting. Irene removed some of the sampler blocks from the bed sheet to use as patterns to make new quilts. But the blocks that were too badly damaged from the wagon wheel's corrosion, she stored away.

When Grandmother died, I inherited the remainder of her cherished quilt block collection. I shared the history of the wagon wheel rusted blocks when I presented each cousin a block as a precious keepsake. I squirreled away four blocks for my children.

Some of the blocks were lovingly framed for display. Unfortunately, one block blew away in the May 3, 1999 tornado in Moore, Oklahoma. One great-grandson traced a pattern from his block and his mom made a quilt using Irene's pattern. Another granddaughter also prepared a pattern from her block to put together a quilt. She then shared the pattern with me so I eventually can create my own quilt. I'm searching for material duplicating the same calicos Grandma used in her original block so that I can recreate my quilt as authentically as possible.

The Sades' homestead remained in the family until recently and was designated an *Oklahoma Centennial Farm* in 1989. I proudly can say that Grandmother's *Centennial Block Collection* documenting Oklahoma's land-run and our family history also has remained in the family and will perpetuate Irene Jane's legacy of love to each succeeding generation.

*"I press on toward the goal to win the prize for which God has called me heavenward in Christ Jesus. . . Join with others in following my example, brothers, and take note of those who live according to the pattern we gave you." Phillipians 3:14, 17*

## *Legacy of the Cast Iron Kettle, Milk Pitcher and Quilt*

*by Ima Jean Thornton*

My grandmother Belle Fossett Hollis of Grove Oak, Alabama, died in 1913, leaving my mother Bronte Hollis, Mabel, and Euclid. The children were reared by their uncle. This picture taken in 1921 is of the red and green appliquéd quilt Grandmother made in the 1800s with Mother at age sixteen standing in front. There were three articles saved for the children as their legacy: a cast iron kettle, blue and white milk pitcher, and this quilt. We still have the milk pitcher. The quilt was cared for by Mabel until Euclid was in his early twenties. Mabel spent two days carefully washing and drying the quilt, then presented it to Euclid to keep for his bride when he married. He was a carefree guy. His bride never saw the quilt.

We've asked Aunt Mabel many times what happened to the quilt. Finally at the beauty shop one day, fed up with our questions, my straitlaced aunt blurted out, "I don't know what happened to the damn quilt!" Since Mabel never had cussed in her life, everyone in the shop cracked up. We knew we'd struck a tender nerve with Grandmother's legacy quilt and never brought it up again.

*"I will not leave you orphans; I will come to you." John 14:18*

# *Carding*

### by Mary Lynn Kotz

Some women in our town played bridge on Monday afternoons. Not my mother. She taught music in schools all day, and private piano lessons at home in the late afternoons and summertime. Sunday and Wednesday evenings after prayer meeting at church and Thursday afternoons at the radio station were hymn time. She led the choir or played the organ, or both at the same time, in her church for seventy-seven years. For Ms. Booth, playing cards was a waste of time.

Carding, as in preparing bolls of cotton for lining a quilt, was another matter. Big rectangular brushes with wire bristles, paired together so that the bristles would mesh and stretch the fluffy lumps into smooth flat sections, allowed us to spread cotton on the carefully-pieced cloth that hung on a bed-size frame from the ceiling of our big second-floor room.

In the Mississippi hills, cotton and quilting were country pursuits not usually undertaken by town-ladies like my mother. But she was an iconoclast—a liberated Tennessee woman who could ride a swift horse, shoot a snake while catching a passel of fish, play Mozart, direct an operetta, or serve a proper tea.

By the time I was old enough to peer over the edge of the quilt frame, she no longer had the time or patience to stitch together the intricate pieces. The Dutch Girl on my bed was her last solo quilt. The actual quilting around the wooden frame was *her* social event. On an autumn Saturday or winter day when school was out, the ladies would assemble at our house on Old Natchez Trace Road, climb the narrow stairs, and take seats in our dining-room chairs to card the cotton.

Beside each chair was a sackful or basketful of loose cotton. I could hear the dull *smack* of the carding-brushes as they met, opening and closing on the cotton like steel jaws. I wanted to play in the soft mass, to help in some way. "Hand me some cotton, Mary," Aunt Mossie would say sweetly. She had patience with children and piecing quilts. Aunt Gertie's rolling laughter, like a melody, would punctuate the ladies' stories. One would begin—something that had happened to her as a child, usually, and another would pick up, telling her own story, or her mother's, or one she'd heard from someone else. They'd mention Roosevelt, WPA, CCC, the hobos who poured out of the trains from Columbus to Greenville, going from door to door asking for work and a meal. Later, they talked about poor Mr. Oglesby next door who sat down on the ground and sobbed when he lost his boy at Pearl Harbor. The topic would wind down, the cotton pulled carefully from the brushes and laid atop the stretched-out quilt-lining.

Then they'd break for lunch. We could smell hot cornbread wafting up from the kitchen, fresh greens and dried or home-"put-up" beans, fried green autumn tomatoes, creamed corn, cooked fruit and salty ham, and somebody's banana pudding or coconut cake—just like Sunday dinner.

The quilt body would hang on the frame for days or weeks, the quilters an interchangeable bunch of sisters-in-law, fellow members of the Women's Missionary Union or Home Demonstration Club, choir members, and neighbors. My mother rounded up her accomplices who now sat around the frame, lifting and poking thread and needle, as they followed the pattern of the quilt-top, thimbles steering the process through the layers of top, carded cotton, and lining. The stories would pick up, more history than gossip.

It was a social event, not unlike the card parties elsewhere in town. The quilting at our house lasted only for a few years. My mother's multitude of tasks—teaching at faraway schools, raising my young brother and a grandchild—kept her too busy. The war ended, and people moved to the cities. Aunt Mossie quilted all her life, even piecing quilts in the nursing home. Aunt Gertie died young, her laughter echoing in my memory.

But quilting parties, I discovered, have resumed in my mother's Baptist church. Now, young apprentices meet there with the Old Hands once a week to quilt, tell stories, talk Bible, and make a splendid work of art to auction off for choir robes or new hymnbooks. With cotton batting now in ready-made rolls, the sound of carding, like my mother's music, is just a memory.

*"Every good gift and every perfect gift is from above, and comes down from the Father of lights, with whom there is no variation or shadow of turning."*
*James 1:17*

*Heavenly Patchwork II---82*

# Dorinda's Coverlid Comes Alive

### by Judy Howard

One cold Saturday morning spent in my favorite pasttime, "estate-saleing," I stumbled upon something that warmed my soul. "Can you believe this beautiful navy and red coverlet survived the Civil War?" I asked Eunice Brooks of Antique House who was conducting the sale. "If only cloth could talk, I'll bet it could tell American history better than any textbook. Wish I knew the story behind it."

"You're in luck," Eunice volunteered. "I just happen to have this envelope. Maybe it will satisfy your curiosity."

After examining the contents I exclaimed, "Thank you, Zella Page, for documenting this blanket in 1943." The coverlid was woven for Agnes Schneider's mother by her mother Dorinda Whicker Stanley at Amo, Indiana in 1854. The enclosure went on to describe how Dorinda had carded, spun and dyed the red and blue wool herself. Her grandfather had hand-whittled the shuttle used in weaving from a single piece of walnut in 1843. The note said that Dorinda had eight children and made each of them a coverlid.

"She no doubt hand-dyed the red wool with the madder plant and blue wool with the indigo they grew on their farm and hand-wove it on their four-harness loom," I told Eunice. I refolded the coverlet, guessing that Dorinda was well-educated and probably taught her daughters to spin, weave and do fine needlework at an early age, as was the custom back then.

Reading on, I learned that Agnes' grandmother Dorinda was born in Old Salem, North Carolina in 1820. Her family had come from England in 1762 and Dorinda's great-grandfather had fought in the Revolutionary War. "Dorinda and Stanley were married in 1844 in Amo, Indiana, after her parents moved there," I told Eunice.

"Praise the Lord. Letters! I've really hit the jackpot!" I exclaimed pulling out old letters found in the family cedar chest. I couldn't wait to get home to further weave together Dorinda's life and the love behind such a pretty keepsake.

> *"O LORD, You are the portion of my inheritance and my cup;"*
> *Psalm 16:5*

# The Quilt that Ran for Land in the Strip

by Carolyn Branch Leonard

My grandmother Matilda "Tillie" (Barr) Branch finished this Lone Star pattern when she was a teenager. The quilt is all pieced in the same material of red and white alternating diamonds and every inch is done by hand —with millions and millions of tiny perfectly-spaced stitches.

When Tillie started her coverlet about 1880, she was a child of ten living on the Nebraska frontier with her German immigrant parents John B. Barr (Johann Baptist Bahr) and Elizabeth (Trautmann) Barr, and Tillie's nine brothers and sisters.

Tillie later described to her children how she wrapped breakable things, like her mother's good china, in the quilt and packed them in a barrel in the Conestoga wagon when they left Nebraska for a new adventure. Only the most valuable items came with the pioneers.

The Barr family lined up with hundreds of other hopeful families near Anthony, Kansas in a two-mile wide strip of land just north of the Cherokee Indian land designated as the outlet to their hunting grounds in Colorado. This area became known as the Cherokee Outlet or Strip. Land speculators and settlers "boomed" or begged loudly to their congressmen to open the excess real estate, and finally the wish was granted. Competition would be heavy for the Outlet's six million acres. Some people slipped over the line illegally and became known as "Sooners." More than 100,000 people infected with "Strip Fever" on September 16, 1893, waited for the gunshot at high noon signaling start of the race. Then, the air filled with shouts and dust as the line broke and all participants ran "hell-bent for leather" for the squares of 160-acre allotments that could accommodate fewer than 40,000 homesteads. Six out of every ten in the race would go home empty-handed.

Tillie and her parents were among the lucky ones who found an unclaimed spot, drove their stake in the ground, and located rocks with the land description on them that marked the corners. The next morning they rode to the Enid Land Office to file their claim.

Across the section from the Barrs' homestead, Will Branch and his 21-year-old orphaned nephew Alpha Curtis Branch, also drove their stakes and defended their land against claim jumpers.

The younger Branch took a shine to the pretty young fraulein. In 1896, they married at Wakita and lived in a sod house at Gibbon. Alf relinquished his claim to that rich farmland and they moved 110 miles west near Buffalo, Oklahoma where they purchased a less valuable relinquishment. The Lone Star quilt traveled by prairie schooner to the new home in 1901 where Alf and Tillie eventually became parents of three sons and one daughter: Carl Wendell, Ernest Samuel, Mabel Irene and Paul Alpha Branch.

This quilted family heirloom has claimed a championship six times in four different states.

Alf Branch died in 1930 and Tillie Branch in 1946. The bed covering was handed down to their son Ernest Branch who detailed the history of the family—and the quilt— on a tape recording before his death in 1969. He left the quilt to me and in 1982 I gave it to my only daughter Judi Leonard Mills who asked me to display it for her in my home in Oklahoma City.

Tillie never used the Lone Star quilt except as a decorative coverlet for special occasions, so even though it is much more than a hundred years old it is still in good condition. The only damage to the fabric (the red print is faded on one point of the star) was probably caused while it was on display in a glass showcase at the Buffalo Museum. Although my grandmother made many other quilts, the Lone Star is the only quilt still around, making it even more precious to me.

*"By faith Abraham obeyed when he was called to go out to the place which he would receive as an inheritance. And he went out, not knowing where he was going. By faith he dwelt in the land of promise as in a foreign country, dwelling in tents . . ."*
*Hebrews 11:8-9*

# Matte's Quilt of Many Colors
### by Delaine Gately

"That's the most fabulous quilt I've ever seen with its bright rainbow of colors," Delaine gasped as Esther unfolded the wedding quilt her mother Matte gave her as she lay dying on her deathbed.

"Mother knew she couldn't live through another harsh winter to see me married, so she hurriedly finished my quilt just before she died in November, 1936," Esther explained.

Born in 1893, Matte grew up on her parents' farm near Enid, Oklahoma. She married a stern man who became a circuit preacher. Matte's first two of seven children died shortly after birth, leaving Matte weak and consumptive.

Though Matte found great joy in quilting, she had to sew alone because her husband thought the gossiping at the bees was sinful when there were farm chores to be done. Matte sacrificed, bartered and traded for fabric for Esther's wedding quilt which was her finest and last quilt. "That quilt was my comfort after Mom died," Esther said. She wrapped up in it and cried herself to sleep many a night. That's why she extracted a promise from Delaine, the wife of Matte's grandson, that she would be the guardian of Esther's quilt and keep it in the family forever.

Three years later, Esther became gravely ill and her friends rushed her to the hospital. Esther died six months later in a nursing home. As Delaine closed Esther's estate, she was devastated that Matte's quilt had disappeared. In a note, Delaine mentioned the missing quilt to the friends who had taken Esther to the hospital, but heard nothing back from them.

Weeks later, one of the friends called and asked if she could drop by. "I didn't want to get your hopes up, but I remembered that Esther wouldn't go to the hospital without her quilt. I went back to the hospital and searched the lost and found and discovered Matte's quilt, wadded up and pushed back in a corner," the dear lady said as she gingerly handed the bundle to Delaine.

The legacy gift of Matte's quilt of many colors will be passed down through each generation along with the heritage of a good and gentle woman. "Matte may have lived a hard and tragic life, but she sure had pizzazz!" Delaine tells everyone when she exhibits her masterpiece. Matte's inner beauty of love was expressed through her magnificent creation. Now only Matte's quilt is left to tell her story.

*"Every good gift and every perfect gift is from above, and comes down from the Father of lights, with whom there is no variation or shadow of turning." James 1:17*

## Civil War Soldier's Survival Gear

*as told by Donna Shutler to Judy Howard*

"Hi, honey," J.C. Shutler said in 1970 as he greeted his wife Donna with a kiss. "Do you remember Maggie, the nurse who's worked with me for thirty years at the Health Department? Maggie asked if you'd like to come over to her house and look at her grandparents' quilts she wants to sell," J.C. continued. "She lost her husband and is retiring and moving to California to be with her daughter."

"You bet," Donna replied. "I'll call her first thing tomorrow."

Arriving at a small house in the oldest part of Muskogee, Oklahoma, Donna was greeted by the seventy-year-old soft-spoken nurse who ushered Donna into her bedroom. Three faded and worn quilts were spread out on the bed. "This red and white Mosaic quilt was responsible for keeping my grandpa alive during the Civil War. Many of the soldiers died of influenza and pneumonia," she explained. Maggie's grandfather had used the quilt as a pallet to sleep on at night. During the day, he tied a rope around each end and draped the quilt around his shoulders to keep him warm like a cloak.

"I'd love to purchase your quilts and promise to give them a good home," Donna said as she wrote her check. "Thanks so much for thinking of me. I'll cherish this Mosaic quilt as if it came from my own grandfather and delight in telling the fascinating story behind it."

*". . . be strong in the Lord and in the power of His might. Put on the whole armor of God, that you may be able to stand against the wiles of the devil." Ephesians 6:10-11*

# Mystery Quilt
*by Judy Howard*

"I don't want anything in my house older than I am," spry Amanda Jane Cumson told me when I asked her why she was selling her grandmother's quilts. "I'm downsizing and won't have room for anything. My next home will be in Rose Hill's mausoleum," she added with a chuckle.

"But don't you have children who would love these beautiful quilts?" I asked.

"Naw, they have absolutely no interest in anything old either. Besides the quilts have no sentimental value. Grandmother Ida couldn't have made them. Why, she couldn't boil water. My grandfather ran a flour mill in Minneapolis and treated her like a princess. Her maid must have made them for her."

After examining the quilts closely in order to purchase them, I noticed "XXXX" sewn in pink thread on two corners of the 1800's Feathered Star quilt. "What in the world is this supposed to be?" I asked the equally puzzled Amanda.

"I have no idea. I've never seen it before."

The mystery of the Xs will haunt each subsequent owner. Was it a secret code, the signature of a maid who couldn't read or write, or a message of love and kisses from the maker? Oh, if quilts could talk, what an enchanting time we'd have gleaning the secrets of our ancestors.

*"But we speak the wisdom of God in a mystery . . .*
*'Eye has not seen, nor ear heard,*
*nor have entered into the heart of man*
*the things which God has prepared*
*for those who love Him.'"*
*1 Corinthians 2:7a, 9*

Comfort Quilts

# Dustin Hoffman Meets Mary Sunshine

### by Bob Annesley

"Bob, did you give Dustin Hoffman my name?" Mary Woodard asked me over the phone in 1988.

"Why yes, Mary. He was captivated by your mischievous grin and bought the "Mary's Sunshine" pen and ink drawing you posed for last winter. You know it took first place at the Red Earth Art Festival," Bob explained. "I hope you don't mind my giving him directions to your home."

After hearing the story of how Mary exhibited her quilts every weekend on the grounds of the old Cherokee capital building in Tahlequah, Dustin and his art director from *Rainman* said they wanted to meet her in person. It's a wonder Dustin found Mary with the vague directions to drive north out of Tahlequah on Highway 82 past the old red barn and turn east at a homestead (which burned down twenty years ago with only a cracked slab and part of a chimney showing). Then follow the dirt trail that winds up into the woods along the creek and ends in a clearing that contains a cabin with abandoned cars tucked into the surrounding trees. An old yellow Buick stacked to the roof with calico will confirm that you've arrived at Mary Adair Woodard's home.

"Well, they found me all right," Mary said, giggling. "And would you believe they bought every quilt I had and ordered enough extras to keep this eighty-year-old quilting for the rest of her life. Thanks to your portrait, I won't have to spend every weekend selling my wares," Mary said.

Bob first met Mary at a Five Civilized Tribes Art Show at the Cherokee Capitol Building where they both were featured artists. Bob and his wife admired and bought a few of Mary's quilts and loved her "purty yellar" backgrounds she was known for. Bob called these quilts "Mary's Sunshine" and used this name for the title of her portrait—one of three in his American Indian Quilters series.

When Mary was five, her mother gave her cloth scraps, a needle, and unknotted thread to practice her stitches. After two years of pulling out Mary's stitches, her mom knotted the thread and gave her real fabric to sew together.

Mary's father fashioned a leather thimble for her tiny fingers out of the tongue of his old shoe. A big event in Mary's life was when her dad loaded the family into the old truck and drove to Sears to buy her first store-bought thimble.

Before Mary passed away in her nineties, she was still sewing her quilts by hand. Since she loved Jesus with a passion, I'm sure she's in heaven now where "Mary's Sunshine" lights up the sky. The beautiful colors in her quilts are blended into the sunrises and sunsets bringing warmth and cheer to all on earth, including Dustin Hoffman.

*"Let not your heart be troubled . . .*
*In my Father's house are many mansions . . .*
*I go to prepare a place for you."*
*John 14:1-2*

## Thoroughly International Millie
### as told by Mildred Nelson to Judy Howard

After eighteen years, Mildred Nelson, age eighty-three, is still pouring her love into U.C.O. International Students and their spouses. They call her mom and she gets thank-you cards year after year proclaiming, "You're the dearest heart there ever was." Bina Ranebenur considers Mildred her adopted mother. Along with other friends and relatives, Bina enjoys Millie's Saturday breakfasts of pancakes, eggs and bacon in Millie's sunny kitchen, lovingly named by an actual sign outside directing traffic to "Millie's Diner."

Millie teaches quilting for an organization called Friendship International, which also offers English, sewing, scrapbooking, cooking, cross-stitching, painting, and citizenship weekly at the Highland Park Baptist Church in Edmond, Oklahoma. Sponsored by six Baptist churches near the University, this group opens each session with Bible reading and devotions. Twice yearly, the international students share their native cuisines from Puerto Rica, Mexico, Germany, Japan, India, Malaysia, Korea, Sri Lanka and China. The highlight of each semester is the night each girl shows and tells what she's learned, as well as giving her spiritual testimonial.

At a recent year-end party, the students asked Millie how she learned to quilt.

"My mother and grandmother taught me to quilt on a frame that pulled down from the ceiling in the clapboard farm house we homesteaded near Prague," Millie answered. "I sewed my daughters' clothing. But I didn't start quilting 'til the 1960's when I made twenty-five double knit crazy quilts. Since then, I've made quilts for fifteen grandkids, fifteen great-grandkids and one great-great-grandchild."

"Show us what you're working on now," several interested quilters begged their modest teacher.

She showed them the Grandmother's Flower Garden quilt she'd spent the last two years hand piecing. "And it will take another year to hand quilt it," she said.

"How do you make those little hexagons come out so precisely?"

She patiently cut a paper pattern, whip stitched the edges together and then removed the paper to everyone's amazement. "My hubby of sixty-three years fishes and gardens," she explained, "leaving me plenty of time to sew and can the vegetables he grows. One year I put up more than 500 pints and quarts."

"Wow! We ought to add another class, canning!" one of the leaders suggested. "But why do you keep on teaching and quilting at age eighty-three?"

"By the grace of God . . . I just praise the Lord for allowing me to continue teaching others the joy of quilting," Millie replied shyly. "To see your faces light up when those scraps turn into beautiful art makes it worthwhile. It's my greatest pleasure to act as substitute Mom for each of you beautiful young women. I wouldn't trade your friendship for the riches in the world."

As I watched Millie with the young students, one thought came to my heart:

> *". . . lay up for yourselves treasures in heaven,*
> *where neither moth nor rust destroys*
> *and where thieves do not break in and steal.*
> *For where your treasure is, there your heart will be also."*
> *Matthew 6:19*

## Two Firsts

*by Gerry Snyder*

My father died when I was six years old. Three years later, my mother remarried and we moved to another city. I had been very close to my grandparents since Mother and I lived with them after my father died. After we moved, my grandparents wrote letters addressed to me with a dime folded into the corner of each letter. They reasoned that this would prompt me to write to them sooner so their next letter would bring another dime.

A dime could buy a lot in 1930. Though I would have preferred a doll or candy, Mother persuaded me to purchase one yard of fabric with each dime. She wanted me to make a Butterfly quilt. So with each dime, I bought one-third yard of three different calicos, enough for three butterflies. I also made butterflies from my outgrown dresses.

On each of the eighteen 12" blocks, using a blanket stitch, Mom and I appliquéd and embroidered a butterfly. We back-stitched the antennae and satin-stitched spots on the wings. Here our project ended.

Fifty-eight years later, friends asked me to join a quilting group. Remembering my Butterfly blocks that I'd made as a child, I pulled them out of my trunk and stitched them together into a top. I then quilted that top. I added a ruffle for the border and, on the quilt's back I sewed a short story of how the quilt came to be. My love for this quilt must have been evident. because the judges awarded my Butterfly quilt first place at that year's county quilt show.

Many happy memories of my grandparents' cunning ways, Mother's tutoring, the fun times with the quilting group, and the joy of winning the blue ribbon for my first quilt are attached to my Butterfly quilt.

A little girl had created the quilt blocks with dreams for the future. While finishing this quilt I prayed that God would enfold those who use it in His loving arms of comfort and protection just as the quilt wrapped them in warmth. I feel snug and secure when I sleep beneath it. Afterall, pleasant memories make good bedfellows!

*"When I remember You on my bed, I meditate on You in the night watches. Because You have been my help, Therefore in the shadow of Your wings I will rejoice. My soul follows close behind You; Your right hand upholds me." Psalm 63:5-7*

# Patchwork Prayers

*by Beverly Cook Sievers*

Abbey, our puppy, was barking and running to her chair to look out the living room window. Irritated at her interruption, I looked up from my favorite pastime of quilting on my Longarm machine and asked, "What is it, Abbey? Is someone at the door?"

I didn't feel like company today. I just wanted to be alone. It had been only a few weeks since my forty-two-year-old son Robert had died from a "silent killer," undiagnosed diabetes. I was savoring his precious memories, and still, asking over and over again "why?"

I looked out the window and saw a big delivery truck driving away. I don't have anything ordered from Fed Ex, I thought. What could it be? I went to the door and discovered a large box addressed to me.

Excited and curious, like a child at Christmas, I brought the cumbersome package inside. The name on the return address was that of a member of the Longarm machine quilting forum, Machine Quilting Professional, of which I'm also a member. I had just recently resubscribed, after being dropped from the list while Robert was sick. I had, however, kept in touch with my one friend in the group by using the hospital computer while Robert was in the hospital. In turn, this special friend had kept the members of the quilting group updated. Robert was in the hospital a long time and finally on life support for ten days before he passed away.

I opened the box as fast as I could, wondering what it was and why this special friend would be sending me anything. What a shock! The first thing I saw was a beautiful white square of cloth embroidered in bright yellow on dark blue, stitched evenly in white. The square was embroidered beautifully and said, "Patchwork Prayers, Made with Love, By MQP friends, for Bev Sievers, In memory of her son, Robert W. Cook September 2003."

By the time I finished reading, I was wiping away tears of intermingled sorrow, memories, joy and wonder. I took the bundle out of the box to discover a beautifully pieced Signature quilt in memory of Robert that my friends of the MQP had made. Red, white, and blue patchwork stars adorned the top of this beautiful quilt, along with personal messages and prayers from various members. I spread the quilt out on the floor in awe and read through my tears what several contributing members had written on their squares.

Words never could express how I felt that day, or even how I felt after that, every time I looked at my Memory quilt. This beautiful example of friendship and fidelity is on my bed, and every night wraps me in warm hugs and memories.

God sends angels in many different ways. I never have seen so many patchwork prayers at once, on one quilt, made especially for Robert and for me. My son will live in my heart forever as well as the healing love and comfort I received from this special gift.

*"Be anxious for nothing, but in everything by prayer and supplication, with thanksgiving, let your requests be made known to God; and the peace of God, which surpasses all understanding, will guard your hearts and minds through Christ Jesus."*
*Philippians 4:6-7*

## Sequel to Healing Hands Quilt
*by Vicki Potts, Sharon Newman's daughter, to Judy Howard*

You may recall my mother Sharon Newman's story featured in *Heavenly Patchwork I* about the quilt made with healing hands for Sharon by the Los Alamos, New Mexico, guild when she was first diagnosed with cancer. In March of 2005, Sharon came to stay with me in Marshall, Texas. On May 25th, she had emergency surgery and as a result of complications she went home to be with the Lord on June 17th.

As my sisters and I looked through her books to find the right words to share at her memorial service, we found her story in *Heavenly Patchwork*. The minister read her story at the service and added the following:

"Sharon had the Healing Hands quilt with her in the hospital. It covered her as she was dying and lifted her spirits. Perfect healing has finally come and she's free of pain. Now, the quilt will be shared by her three daughters. Any time someone in the family is ill or hurting, Sharon's quilt will be sent to provide comfort, healing, and cheer once again."

We smiled through our tears as we heard Mom's words read at the end of her story, "I am currently free of cancer, and daily praise the Lord for His healing strength and for the sacrificial love stitched in my quilt to comfort and console me during my times of greatest need."

*"Death is swallowed up in victory." I Corinthians 15:54*

# Anna's Daddy Pillow

### by Esterita Austin

During the Long Island blizzard of 1977, my husband Tom and I were house-bound, unable to go to work for a week. I relished the delightful time spent playing in my studio. Our first anniversary was rapidly approaching and this was the perfect opportunity to make a gift for Tom.

I had a great photo of Tom sitting at a picnic table leaning forward with his chin resting on his palm and the biggest Cheshire grin on his face. I painted Tom's face on a piece of natural muslin and did his torso in sepia tones. I then transformed the painting into a quilted life-size pillow.

On the eve of our anniversary, I tiptoed downstairs and propped the pillow on the couch. The next morning when my bleary-eyed husband sauntered downstairs for his morning wake-up coffee was he ever startled to see another Tom on the couch grinning right back at him! We both enjoyed that little joke.

The life-like pillow remained on the couch for many years, surprising visitors. During that time our family grew. First Peter, then Bennett, and finally Anna was born. Sadly, when Anna turned one, Tom was diagnosed with cancer and, shortly after, passed away.

It was a traumatic time for us. Anna latched onto that pillow and wouldn't let go. She slept with "her daddy" for two years. During that second year, she occasionally forgot the pillow when she went up to bed. Without fail, on those nights she'd awaken in the middle the night and wail, "I want my daddy!" It was heartbreaking for me. Of course I would quickly run downstairs to retrieve the pillow.

I never could have imagined how much comfort and peace my quilted pillow would provide for a toddler or how God would use it to heal our grieving hearts. Anna is a college student now, and the pillow is back on the couch, smiling up at us.

*"As one whom his mother comforts, so I will comfort you;"*
*Isaiah 66:13a*

# The Love Quilt

*by Jean Lewis*

I slowly shook my head, trying to focus my eyes. A deep fog enveloped me, but I heard whispered voices close by. Off and on, I felt the cool cloth someone placed on my brow. Who was it? Where was I? What's happening to me? I was cold and shivering. Then, amazingly, warmth came over me and I slept far into the night.

Later, I opened my eyes to behold the face of my beloved husband. He smiled and told me he loved me. "What's happened?" I asked.

"You've had scarlet fever, but you're going to be okay now," he replied. "The kids can come in as soon as Jack feeds the cows and Marcie finishes the dishes. We've kept them away on purpose. Old Doc Harvey said you needed lots of rest to get well. So, lie back and take it easy."

My senses slowly returned and I began to worry about our farm and the many chores it took to keep it running. I listened to the wind whistling between the logs of our walls.

Weeks later, I tried to sit up in bed. My head "swam" for a minute, but soon cleared.  Looking around my room, I could see evidence of the loving care I had received . . .  the white pitcher full of the cool water from the creek, the clean rags by the wash basin, the quilt that covered me . . . .

The quilt!  Where had that come from? I didn't remember ever seeing it before. Looking closer, I found big, uneven quilting stitches like my mother fussed at me for taking when I was first learning. I saw a square of fabric from the plaid shirt I had made Jim last Christmas. How proud he was. Another square was from the faded hem of my one and only church dress. How I had loved wearing it to the church every Sabbath.

Could it be? Yes. Another square was from my white calico wedding dress. Now, I knew that someone in this household had been in my rag box and my good scrap bag I kept under my bed. I was getting excited trying to discover the source of the squares in this poorly sewn quilt. There was the wool plaid I had used to make a horse blanket. Then, my eyes fell upon a black challis square . . . my momma's burial dress. She died young and suddenly, having endured the hard life on the plains the best she could. I had to stay up late the night before her funeral to make this dress. The neighbor ladies had laid her out on our kitchen table, covered her face with a wet paste made of soda and water to keep her skin soft and white for the funeral.

Quickly, I found another square that I could not recognize at first. Was it from a dishrag? No. I remembered seeing that print on a feed sack not long ago. What happened to the feed? I saw a piece from Marcie's birthday dress, one from Aunt Bessie's apron, one from the calico curtain material I bought with egg money. Did I now have a square hole in my curtain? Surely not!

My body was growing tired, so I scrunched down in the feather bed, drew the quilt up to my chin and slept.

Later, I learned that Marcie had been working secretly for some months on this quilt up in her loft bedroom. It was to be my Christmas gift. She had gathered scraps from every source imaginable, and some not imaginable. I knew she had borrowed my needle and some thread, but I did not question it. Christmas gifting was a secretive time for the whole family, as each one made do with what he had. When Marcie saw me shivering that day, she ran up the loft stairs to her room and pulled out the almost finished quilt from under the cot. She quickly made the last stitches and raced downstairs to have Pa place it over me.

Was it the quilt that kept me warm and brought healing to my body? Or was it the love that went into making it?

*". . . not that we loved God, but that He loved us and sent His Son to be the propitiation for our sins. Beloved, if God so loved us, we also ought to love one another." 1 John 4:10-11*

## Doctor Takes Quilt to Hospital

*as told by Dr. Wilson and Betty Mahone to Judy Howard*

"Did you see what I saw?" Nurse Maple asked Nurse Downy with surprise in her voice. "Or are my eyes playing tricks on me?"

"It's certainly no trick, and that is a real quilt tucked around Dr. Mahone."

It's not often you see an antique handmade quilt adorning a bed in a hospital. But Wilson Mahone at eighty-nine years is spoiled. He grew up sleeping under his grandmother's handmade quilts.

When the nurses asked him about the quilt, he replied, "I can't imagine going to bed without my Chin Quilt. It's a little bit of heaven—a comforting touch from God as He wraps me in His love. When I snuggle it around my head, I feel safe and secure and fall immediately into a peaceful sleep." And with that, he did.

Besides admitting he was spoiled, Dr. Mahone spun marvelous tales of his past. "Born in a dug-out in Arkansas, my mom was so tiny, her parents transported her in a shoe box when they traveled to the Indian Territory with their belongings conveyed in a covered wagon," he told Nurse Maple one afternoon. "Granddad was the Horatio Algiers of his day, establishing a general store later in Custer City, Oklahoma. At one end, he stocked groceries. At the other

end, he sold dry goods, including feed and flour, packaged in those great fifty pound and one hundred pound calico fabric sacks later used in his wife's quilting."

He told the nurses how he remembered churning butter and gathering eggs on stays with Grandma, and sleeping under her wonderfully warm quilts. He loved visiting when she had quilting bees at her house. Quilting kept his grandmother's fingers nimble in useful activity and her mind engaged in pleasant memories after her husband died. The quilting bees were her only social activity and kept her connected and interacting with neighbors and friends.

"How fascinating," Nurse Maples interjected whenever Wilson paused to catch his breath. She also asked questions about Dr. Mahone's father.

"Dad left his Georgia home at age sixteen to work on the railroad. He kept moving further west as the railroad expanded and became the telegrapher at Custer City, where he met Mama. When the old crank-type moving pictures became popular between 1907 and 1915, Dad bought a projector, rented film and started showing movies in a second floor space over a store building. He borrowed chairs from the funeral home."

Dr. Mahone's parents moved to Cordell where he was born in 1915. There they opened a theater and later one in Hobart. "You might say I spent my childhood at the picture shows," he said. "I sold tickets and played the piano for the early talkies in the 1920s. We almost got booted out of town when we opened for Sunday matinees. I still have the ticket box for Premium Night Drawings at the theater when they gave away dishes as a promotional. That's when tickets cost ten cents."

Wilson's wife Betty arrived in time to add her two cents worth. "I remember my parents driving me from Durant to Dallas to see *Gone with the Wind* in 1935. Movies were hugely important during the

Depression. I dated the fire chief's son and since his family got free tickets, I often went with him. The Saturday late night previews were my favorite. We cried so hard in *Dark Victory* with Betty Davis that we didn't want it to end because everyone would see our red eyes and noses."

"What was it like growing up in the Depression?" Nurse Maple asked.

"Mom often prepared plates of food for the beggars who came to our back porch. I went to grade school with Indian kids who were bused in from the Oklahoma Presbyterian College campus where they lived as wards of the state. We had black household help who lived in our home Monday through Friday. Mom took them home every Friday night to Colbert since Durant was a Jim Crow town and didn't allow black residents."

Betty's dad was an independent oil jobber and supplied gas and oil products across Southeastern Oklahoma for Tidewater and later Phillips 66. "I worked for Dad every summer," Betty said. "My job was pasting the gasoline stamps from WW11 rationing books and trying to reconcile the records with the state." When Betty went to OU, she took her share of meat and sugar stamps to the sorority to purchase her food.

"Did your family quilt too?" the nurse asked Betty.

"I remember the quilting bees at my grandparents' General Store in Whitlock, Tennessee," Betty said. "They set up permanent quilting frames in the building adjacent to their store." Even though her mom hated to quilt, she loved the socializing around the quilting frame on every visit back home. "And I loved playing beneath the quilting frame, sitting under there hidden away eating foolish pie made with fresh strawberries and meringue topping," Betty finished.

"And now you know why my children brought my favorite worn, but still beautiful old quilt to the hospital to make me feel right at home with the comforts, cheer, and warm memories that only my cuddly quilt can provide," Wilson concluded.

Though none of their grandparents' quilts survived, Wilson and Betty's love and appreciation for beautiful quilts motivated them to collect quilts throughout their married life. They use them daily for warm cover, even in hospital stays. They also decorate with them and give them to their children as their legacy of love.

> *"I lay down and slept; I awoke, for the LORD sustained me.*
> *I will not be afraid..."*
> *Psalm 3:5 NKJ*

# *Twister Brings a Whirlwind of Blessings*

*by Judy Howard*

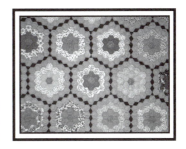

People arrive at Buckboard Antique Quilts on everything from motorcycles, bicycles, vintage hot rods, and conventional cars—but never before a stretch limousine. Late one spring afternoon about closing time, I was paying bills and praying for one big sale to meet the monthly expenses. I heard a motor and a car door slam and grumbled under my breath, "It's probably just another last-minute shopper who will make me late for church and won't buy a thing." I peeked out the lace curtains to behold the impossible. A chauffeur was holding open the door for a very grand lady to step out of the longest limo I'd ever seen.

I welcomed this sophisticated lady into the shop and asked how I could be of assistance. "I'm Connie Tavel, in town with Helen Hunt as her partner and agent during the filming of *Twister*. You wouldn't believe the near calamities we've experienced chasing your Oklahoma tornadoes," this lady answered, adjusting a large diamond pendant around her neck. "It's been a perilous adventure. If it hadn't been for Annie, the stunt girl, Helen wouldn't have survived the flying Big Mac trucks and John Deere tractors."

"Oh yes, I've met sweet little Annie Ellis with the Goldilocks voice," I said, folding up my bills folder and shoving it into a drawer. "She came in several times to buy quilts for her mother," I told Ms. Tavel. "I've never seen anyone so anxious to retire to live a normal life and raise a family. My heart broke for her each time she told of her near-death experiences and fears," I said.

I helped Connie select a Grandmother's Flower garden quilt for her mother's birthday I was to ship to her Wilshire Boulevard address in Beverly Hills. Connie used my mail order service for her mother's next birthday and Christmas gifts, so I've never seen that limo again, but I covered the bills that month thanks to the *Twister* filming.

Wonders never cease in the surprises God has for His precious children. He rewards us spiritually, along with a few material blessings, and knows just when we need a windfall of encouragement to keep us going.

> *"Do not fear, little flock, for it is your Father's good pleasure to give you the kingdom." Luke 12:32 NKJ*

# The Cuddle Quilt

*by Betty C. Hatcher*

"But how will Maudie ever keep her relatives straight?" Auntie Nancy Everheart asked Trigg and Jess, the parents of the recently adopted seven-year-old child from Kazakhstan. Trigg and Jess had spent three months in Kazakhstan and had adopted two eight-month-old boy and girl babies, Eli and Ivy. At that time, they believed their family was complete. And then they fell in love with Maudie's picture. Once more they traveled to Kazakhstan to bring her home to northern Colorado.

After considerable thought, Nancy had an inspiration.

She gathered photographs of relatives, twelve of them, and had them printed on pale blue fabric to make a quilt for Maudie. Trigg was delighted. At cuddle time, wrapped in the quilt, Maudie could learn stories about her new relatives. When she met them, they would not be strangers.

Nancy's idea snowballed. Folks who saw the family pictorial quilt were inspired with new uses. One woman made a quilt for her mother who struggled with cancer. Another lady created a picture quilt including the grandchildren for a proud grandma. Someone suggested such a quilt might help an Alzheimer's patient hold onto the memory of faces awhile longer.

Nancy was amazed at how her idea of the family album quilt created for her newly adopted niece expanded to help others. Maudie loved her cuddle quilt. Now happy and fluent in English in her new home, she comfortably greets cousins, aunts and uncles whose pictures graced her cuddle quilt.

*"Fear not, for I have redeemed you;*
*I have called you by your name; You are Mine.*
*When you pass through the waters, I will be with you;*
*and through the rivers, they shall not overflow you.*
*When you walk through the fire, you shall not be burned,*
*nor shall the flame scorch you.*
*For I am the LORD your God . . . ."*
*Isaiah 43:1-3a*

# The Millionaire

### by Linda Morton

As a young girl, I loved watching *The Millionaire* on TV, about an anonymous donor who each week gave a family $1,000,000 in the midst of some tragedy. I've often dreamed what I'd do with $1,000,000 . . . or better yet, what it would be like to be that anonymous donor.

Though I'll never have a $1,000,000 to bestow, I do enjoy giving quilts to unsuspecting people. Just as the families on *The Millionaire* cried or screamed with uncontrollable joy upon receiving such a life-changing donation, I want the recipients of my quilt to express their joy upon receiving my labor of love.

Injured in an automobile accident, Nancy was a shut-in for many weeks. When I surprised her with an appliquéd tea pot lap quilt I'd created in her favorite colors, she was thrilled beyond words. In Nancy's thank-you-note she wrote, "I don't know what I did to deserve such a gift."

Five-year-old Bryson was scheduled for surgery and everyone at our Memorial Road Church of Christ was praying for his quick recovery. I just knew he would benefit from the comfort of a quilt, so I made him one with race cars. With the encouragement of his mother, Bryson named each car. He was shy with me, but I could tell he loved the unexpected quilt.

Rita, Bryson's mother, told me in her thank-you-note that Bryson wanted to be under the quilt all the time because it "made him more comfortable." She also wrote, "Your quilt has blessed our whole family and has brought Bryson great joy and comfort. We are greatly moved by the love you've shown to a little boy you hardly know."

I've made quilts for babies at the Oklahoma Welfare Department, sent quilts overseas, and have given quilts to orphans. I rarely hear from these recipients, but I rejoice imagining the joy the child receives when he unwraps my unexpected treasure. The hundreds of hours I've spent quilting is worth more to me than a million dollars. My time is an investment in the happiness of others.

Though I could tell you many more stories, you'll only understand if you've given away something of value . . . if you've sacrificed something to benefit others. This blessing of giving comes from God Himself, who gave His only Son as a sacrifice for our sins.

> *"And remember the words of the lord Jesus, that He said, 'It's more blessed to give than to receive.'"*
> *Acts 20:35*

# Going Home

*by Linda Carlson*

"I wanna go home," my mother-in-law kept repeating during Sunday dinners at her daughter Jean and son-in-law Stan's home. Coping with senile dementia was not what Doretta Carlson prayed her last years would be.

"Do you mean North Town Village, or the house on Keystone or on Military?" Jean asked.

"No" Doretta would always replay. "I wanna go home."

The night before Doretta passed away, Jean and Stan visited her in the Alzheimer's living center. Doretta was excited. Grinning with glee she announced, "I'm going home now! Mom and Sis are waiting for me."

After eating dinner and listening to her favorite childhood hymns, Doretta peacefully fell asleep. In the middle of the night, she went home to Mom and Sis, her father-in-law Fritz and her four brothers. Doretta's lucid conversation that last night was a miracle since Doretta had experienced great difficulty forming coherent thoughts, much less complete sentences for the past few years.

I made Doretta's casket quilt in three days, finishing the binding as we drove the nearly seven hours to Omaha, Nebraska. To ease my heavy heart, I quilted to soothe my soul, and once again cover her with the labor of my hands.

As a quilting workshop leader, I committed to create a small quilt to travel in Alzheimer's awareness quilt shows. The quilts will be auctioned to raise funds for Alzheimer's research in an effort spearheaded by Ami Simms of Michigan. My plan is to sit in Doretta's wheelchair covered with the lap quilt I made featuring photo transfers of the homes where she's lived. It's the least I can do to help eradicate "Old Timer's Disease."

*"Let not your heart be troubled . . .*
*In My Father's house are many mansions . . .*
*I go to prepare a place for you . . .*
*that where I am, there you may be also."*
*John 14:1-3*

# The Butterfly Quilt
### by Delita Caudill

When I saw the picture of a Butterfly quilt in the March/April 2001 issue of Fons and Porter's *For the Love of Quilting*, I immediately thought of my mother's quilt she'd made when I was very young. I remember being fascinated with the colorful butterflies she pieced, appliquéd and embroidered onto white muslin squares. Mother warned me to handle the butterflies carefully so they wouldn't ravel or stretch and to keep my hands clean.

I saw the planning that went into piecing the squares together around the center block and the border that was measured so carefully, because material was costly and times were hard. That was in 1942 during wartime and at the end of the Depression. Little did we know just how much harder those times were to be. My dad was crippled as a boy and his lame leg made it impossible for him to earn a decent living with doctors' bills to pay. Mother worked in the fields, shocking feed, chopping and pulling cotton to help feed the three of us. But she didn't believe in being idle and continued her quilting even after a hard day's working.

I remember the times my cousins and I sat near the quilting frames and listened to the grownups talk. We dreamed of the time when we would be allowed to sew, especially to play with scissors and wear a thimble. Mother explained that only God could create perfection, although we should do our best. As an act of humility, she always left something undone, turned wrong or made a deliberate mistake she called a devil's eye to make sure she didn't steal God's glory.

One by one, Mama's quilts disappeared. We kept only the heavy coarse quilts made from old work clothes. I suspect she sold her brightly colored quilts to put food on the table. I still have some quilt tops made later. But once those quilting days stopped, they never started again, and the quilt tops I have are drab and plain compared to the Butterfly quilt I remembered.

I called the publishers of the magazine in Alabama, asking about the Butterfly quilt. I told them the story of Mother's quilt and how she made sure she didn't do a perfect job.

"That quilt was from a store in Oklahoma City," they replied. "We had to display it on an angle in the magazine to hide an unfinished block in the bottom right corner."

That store was later identified as Buckboard Antique Quilts.

Could it have been my mother's quilt? I like to think it was, but I'll never know. I only know that to a little girl that Butterfly quilt was the most beautiful thing I'd ever seen. And in my eyes it was perfect, despite what mother said.

*"He is the Rock, His work is perfect;*
*for all His ways are justice,*
*a God of truth and without injustice;*
*righteous and upright is He."*
Deuteronomy 32:4

## *Passion for Collecting*
### *by Dee Wojciechowski*

Many falls ago when I was first married, I went to an antique show with my mother and spotted a quilt top that won my heart. I wanted that top so badly that I never stopped talking about it.

Christmas morning, we were unwrapping presents at Mom's house. She handed me a gift from her. Ripping off the bow and red foil paper I spied a corner of blue and red calico fabric. "Why does this look so hauntingly familiar?" I asked her. Unfolding it, I realized it was the quilt top I had coveted several months before.

With tears welling, I gave Mom a happy hug. "I'm overwhelmed that you surprised me with my heart's desire. How did you sneak it out without my knowing? And how did you keep your secret every time I kicked myself for not buying it?"

Mom's caring gift started my life-long passion for collecting quilts. I eventually quilted the top she gave me and I have bought many quilts since that time. But that blue and red top always will be one of my favorites, especially since Mother passed away twenty years ago. I am captivated by the patterns, colors and feel of vintage fabrics and am forever indebted to Mother for surprising me with that first quilt.

*"For the wages of sin is death,*
*but the gift of God is eternal life in Christ Jesus our Lord."*
*Romans 6:23*

# A Quilt from My Angel

*by Emily Elizabeth Buchanan*

"Are you coming back?" asked a friend on the phone from the orphanage.

"Yes. Mrs. Hubbard said to be back by the twenty-eighth."

"No. She said she told you to be back by the eighteenth. They've already given your room away," Bonnie responded.

My arm holding the phone went limp as I heard Bonnie talking, but I wasn't listening. Oh no! It can't be. My room—gone? That was all I had in the whole world. What would I do now? Where would I go? I had lived in an orphanage since I was eleven years old. I was fifteen and a half, soon to be sixteen. Sixteen and homeless. I felt as lost and scared as a little child separated from her mother in a supermarket. I remembered what happened when other girls left the orphanage— their belongings were divvied up among the remaining girls who cast lots for what they wanted.

My sister Ruby and I were visiting Uncle Benny and Aunt Loyola for the summer, the first time in eight years we had seen any of my mother's family. Still in a state of shock, I managed to relay the phone message to Aunt Loyola. She gave me a quizzical look that said, *So, what's the problem*? Then she graciously announced, "You can live with us," as she took my hand to console me. That would be no small feat. With eight children of their own, they recently had adopted a baby, and had adopted my younger sister and brother when Mother died. With eleven children already, she still invited my sister Ruby and me to live with them without even consulting Uncle Benny. She just knew we needed a place to live, and opened her home to us, confident God would provide. And He did.

We made many wonderful memories. We played tennis every Saturday morning before returning home to do our chores. We cleaned house from top to bottom and baked yummy cupcakes and cookies to host an occasional party with music and dancing for our friends. Aunt Loyola videotaped us in our revelry— the highlight of my childhood. The memories are etched on my mind and heart.

Life has taken us along divergent paths, but we keep in close contact. Aunt Loyola is an angel to me. Without regard for herself, she took me in and loved me as her own. "Always remember that you are one of my children, and I love you very much," she reminded me on every visit as she lovingly brushed my curly hair away from my face with her hands as if I were six years old.

On a recent visit, Loyola gave me a wool quilt she made just for me. She knew how much I loved wool and that I would appreciate the gift since I was a quilter myself.

"Oh, Auntie, thank you so much. I love the way you pieced these beautiful black, blue, grey, and tan blocks together. And these red strings you used for tying it stick up just like little hearts," I said as I wiped away the tears and gave her a happy hug.

But more than my love for wool and this quilt, I loved Loyola for providing me a home and a purpose to go on. Every time I wrap up in its warm comfort, I'll remember that I'm one of her children. I'll always treasure this tangible reminder of her faithful sacrificial love.

> *"I will never leave you nor forsake you*
> *So we may boldly say:*
> *The LORD is my helper; I will not fear.*
> *What can man do to me?"*
> Hebrews 13:5-6

## It's a Small World

*as told by Kay and Don Gilbert to Judy Howard*

I always enjoyed visiting with Kay and Don Gilbert, owners of Kay's Antiques in Tulsa, Oklahoma, when they came into my Buckboard Antique Quilt shop in Oklahoma City. This Saturday's visit was no exception and yielded a shock for us. Kay and Don are veteran quilt collectors with a stash of more than one hundred quilts, and are always looking for "whatever talks to them" to decorate their 1935 English cottage located in one of Tulsa's historic neighborhoods.

Both Kay and Don spotted a striking black and yellow-bordered postage stamp Trip Around the World quilt at the same instant." Oh my gosh!" Kay screamed. "Look at the provenance on this quilt. It was made in Mountain Home, Arkansas, in the late 1920's where Mom and Dad lived when they were first married." Back then Kay's family would have known the quilter because that wide-spot-in-the road couldn't have had more than fifty residents. "We definitely need to add this to our collection even though it's not in perfect condition," Kay told Don, "and besides it's such a stunning graphic work of art."

Kay went on to describe the rush of fond memories and the family's life during the Depression that the quilt from Mountain Home evoked. "Mom made only one quilt during her lifetime, though we were always surrounded by family quilts. She loved to embroider, so she created a forty-eight state bird and flower top and quilted it by hand."

Fingering other quilts as she talked, Kay told me, "I loved the Grandmother's Flower Garden that covered my feather mattress when I was growing up. My five sisters and brothers always tormented me by sitting and jumping on that feather mattress because they knew I couldn't tolerate 'butt prints.' So I'd have to get the mattress fluffer out each time to repair the damage.

Kay's dad came from a family of twelve children from a farm in Southern Missouri in the Ozarks with lots of functional scrap bag quilts. Kay found her mom and dad's sweet love letters with song lyrics like *Wings of a Dove* in with the scraps.

"Don is just as sentimental and sweet as my dad," Kay explained. "Don's always surprising me with a quilt for birthdays, Valentine's day, Christmas and anniversaries. He's as enthusiastic about collecting quilts as I am and invents novel ways to display them like attaching towel racks at the top of doors from which to hang them.

Kay knew that the Mountain Home quilt would have a special place in her heart forever because of the connection it made with her parents and the fond memories of her childhood.

Kay and Don took their bundled up wonder, thanking me for caring enough to investigate and include the history of each quilt. "The information makes each quilt spring alive and tell a story that brings past and present together," Kay concluded as she wiped away a tear and walked out the door with her new prize.

> *"I have loved you with an everlasting love;*
> *Therefore with loving kindness I have drawn you."*
> *Jeremiah 31:3*

# Grandmother's Quilt Fought the Goblins

*by Tonya Shook*

Seconds before a thunderous clap, silver and blue jagged fingers streaked the night sky, sending brilliant flashes through the farmhouse. It was hot and stuffy under the quilt, but safe. Light split the sky once again.

My grandmother told me before she left, "I'll be back after I milk the cows. You go nitey-night and I'll tuck you in later."

But sleep wouldn't come. The lightning cunningly waited until Grandmother left before revealing its plan to eat me alive. I clutched the quilt and slid off the iron bed to seek refuge under the dining room table. I was positive the fortified walls of the quilt protected children from the voracious appetites of dragons of the night. The soft cloth against my skin provided imaginary parental arms to keep out noisy monsters.

I had watched Grandmother cut thousands of fabric squares, triangles and octagons without knowing a name for her patience-and-love message. Quilts always existed in this homesteaded Oklahoma farmhouse as evidenced by a photo in the family album of Mama standing next to her grandmother who held up a newly made quilt. That quilt was now threadbare, but lovingly stored in the closet.

Such picture memories gave comfort in the stuffy space under one of the newer masterpieces. Mama also must have sought protection under Grandmother's quilts when she was small. With that thought, I drifted off to sleep in the arms of my comforter under the table listening to the howling storm and for Grandma's step at the door.

> *"Surely He shall cover you with His feathers,*
> *and under His wings you shall take refuge:*
> *His truth shall be your shield and buckler.*
> *You shall not be afraid of the terror by night,*
> *Nor of the arrow that flies by day,"*
> *Psalm 91:4-5*

*Healing Quilts*

# A Time to Quilt

*by Mary Ann Tate*

I grew up sleeping under Grandma's quilts. She made me a special Sunbonnet Sue quilt which I still love even though it's tattered and torn. Mother stitched our clothing until I took over after excelling in seventh grade Home Economics. I loved sewing. I watched Mom save scraps from our clothes and pack them away to "make a quilt some day."

Though I inherited those scraps and the desire to quilt, I'd never watched the process. Overwhelmed by the thought of putting together those little pieces, I stuck to sewing clothes on a Bernina 830 I purchased in 1978.

In 1996 as I pursued my life's dream of singing in a band, disaster struck. Tests revealed I had a neuromuscular disease called myasthenia gravis. I progressed from singing four-hour shows three to five nights a week to barely being able to speak, walk, swallow or breathe. I spent three years in bed or a wheelchair trying to climb out of a very deep hole called despair.

During that time, God was teaching me patience. I only had energy to be out of bed a few minutes at a time. I learned that most television was not worth watching except for HGTV's *Simply Quilts* which I flipped on for every episode.

After two years I felt so desperate to make a quilt, I vowed to do anything to accomplish my goal. With a book from the library, X-ray film, a marker to trace the pattern, and lots of perseverance, I began recreating Grandma's Sunbonnet Sue quilt in ten-minute sessions at the sewing machine. I'm preserving Grandma's legacy so lovingly stitched by hand more than half a century ago. My quilt will be made to look like the old, but created through the technology of the twenty-first century.

Taking the scraps of Mom's fabric collection, snippets of my time, bits and pieces of my energy, and lots of courage and faith, God is stitching everything together to make me whole and healthy again. I'm fulfilling Mother's dream at last. Quilting has given me small goals to accomplish, a passion and reason to live, and new quilting buddies to share the adventure with.

*"To everything there is a season, A time for every purpose under heaven: ... and a time to sew;" Ecclesiastes 3:1&7*

# Cotton Pickin' Quilter

### as told by Opal Baum

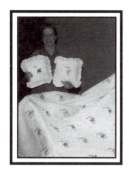

"A week at the beach on the outer banks of North Carolina? You know I'd love to go!" spry eighty-eight-year-old Opal Baum gleefully responded to her daughter's invitation. "How soon do we leave?" Even though living alone for the last twenty-five years, Opal delights in traveling around the country. She's even been to Hawaii and three times to Alaska.

Opal also delights in quilting for her large family and for others for a little extra spending money. Once at the beach, when everyone else applied sunblock and headed for the water, Opal pulled out her needle and thread from her beach bag to complete a hand-pieced block. Her granddaughter asked, "Grandma, why do you love to quilt so much?"

Opal told her this story:

"Quilting is a great alternative to picking cotton, which is what I spent my childhood doing on my parents' farm in Stevens County between Velma and Comanche, Oklahoma. Mama and I always had a quilt in the frame to let down from the ceiling hooks whenever we had a spare minute from baking bread, tending the vegetable garden, milking the cows, canning, cooking, cleaning and sewing. Besides a necessity to keep from freezing in our drafty clapboard home, quilting was our way of unwinding and bonding to create a little beauty from the scraps of our lives for our dismal surroundings."

Opal's family didn't have luxuries like running water or electricity or a Super Wal-Mart down the street. They lived eighteen miles from the nearest general store and there was no money to spend on toys, clothes, Christmas gifts or food. "We grew everything we needed, or else traded milk and eggs for it," Opal told her granddaughter, remembering how thrilled she was when her daddy took the first bale of cotton to town every fall to trade for one pair of school shoes for each of the children.

Opal had time over that beach week to tell her granddaughter about their big community Christmas tree and pie suppers their two-room school sponsored each year to raise money for a stocking for each child. These stockings held one apple, orange, piece of candy and a few nuts. "The Christmas stocking was a huge treat I dreamed about year long," Opal told her granddaughter, adding that if they were lucky, her parents might give each one of them a pair of socks for a Christmas gift.

The question remained though. "So why do you work so hard quilting now, Grandma?"

Opal explained how she had three commissioned quilts to finish before Thanksgiving, plus lots of handmade Christmas gifts for the Sunday school party she hosts each year. Opal clarified that quilting had become her passion—her hobby to keep her hands occupied in a useful activity. "Besides, it's therapeutic to keep my fingers from becoming arthritic. I thank the good Lord everyday for giving me good health and the ability to live a productive independent life even at my age," Opal concluded, realizing anew how quilting feeds her soul with beauty, peace and happiness and affords her a time to pray that these quilts will bring God's comfort and love to those who use them.

*"Even to your old age, I am He, and even to gray hairs I will carry you! I have made, and I will bear; even I will carry, and will deliver you." Isaiah 46:4*

## Covered by the Almighty
### *as told by Freda Correll to Judy Howard*

Born in 1898, Ola Eargle Hamilton left her family's small cotton farm in Little Mountain, South Carolina as a young woman. She moved to Atlanta to learn the millinery business. She fell in love with a city slicker in the railroad business. When Ola and her city boy were courting in 1920, she took him home to introduce him to her family. He was kidded unmercifully for tromping through her homestead cotton fields wearing his new white shoes and spats. Nonetheless, the family graciously accepted him into the family.

Over the years, especially during the months Ola was pregnant with her nine children, she passed the time piecing together scraps from her little girls' dresses into a YoYo quilt coverlet. Although Ola never finished the quilt, her daughter Freda Correll finally did, and sold it in her textile shop, My Favorite Things in Pineville, North Carolina.

Freda recalls Ola's making gingham sunbonnets with rickrack trim for the cotton pickers back home. "Years later at the nursing home, Mom was still making those cotton-picking sunbonnets and selling them for $17 until her death at ninety-seven. Not once would she discount the price," Freda said, chuckling, "not even to me!"

*"O God the LORD, the strength of my salvation, You have covered my head in the day of battle." Psalm 140:7*

# At Home Again

### by Anna Sterling Farris

Five minutes isn't a lot of time. Yet it's enough time to hear the explosion that forever slammed shut 168 coffins—to feel the thunderous tremor that would rumble around the world—to lose everything one has in life.

"In five minutes, how can I possibly collect all I need for daily living?" I asked my mother two weeks after the April 19, 1995, bombing of the Murrah Building in Oklahoma City. "And how can I carry everything in two plastic trash bags?" Tenants of the Regency Apartments were allowed five minutes to return to their rooms to salvage their possessions.

I lived one-half block from the mangled ruins of the Murrah Building and my former place of employment in the Journal Record Building. Worldwide media, television cameramen, and curious onlookers lined crowded sidewalks. I winced at the haunting devastation.

The Regency probably would be condemned and razed along with everything left inside. The building was structurally unsound and too dangerous to allow much movement inside. I planned my strategy while waiting for the tenants of the twelfth floor to be called.

"I hope I'm able to salvage a few pictures and the two quilts Grandma Hattie made," I told my mother, remembering one of Grandmother's two-week visits. When I was only four, she taught me to embroider an entire flower cutout onto an armchair doily. When she visited, she always brought her current quilt block project in a tapestry satchel. How could I let the precious things Grandma Hattie created be destroyed with the building? Losing my Dutch Doll and Lemoyne Star quilts would be like losing family members or old friends.

"If you experienced an emergency situation and had to leave in a hurry, what would you take with you?" was the question posed to my prayer group the night before the bombing. It never occurred to me that I would be forced to make that decision.

When it was finally my turn, armed guards and police escorted our group up to the twelfth floor. There would be only enough time to collect necessities and small valuables. One of the guards pried open my door, then sternly cautioned, "You have five minutes, ma'am."

I was not prepared for the scene of destruction that hit me nor for the hurried pace the officers demanded. Glass covered everything—jagged fragments poked haphazardly out of wood furniture. I headed to the bathroom closet.

"Four minutes!" I heard from the hallway.

I frantically raked prescriptions and clothes into the bags.

"Two minutes!" The guard was practically standing over me. I crunched across glass toward the closet where my quilts were stored. Everything was jumbled—I didn't see them anywhere.

"Ma'am, we've got to go—it's too dangerous to be in here very long."

"Sir, please . . . please, you don't understand. I need to get my valuables. Family pictures, Grandma's quilts—they can't be replaced—they're priceless!" I pleaded.

"Let's go," his partner boomed from the hall.

"I'm sorry, ma'am," the guard said gently with a softened look in his eyes. "There's just not time."

I gulped back tears and left, overwhelmed at the thought of such overall loss. How quickly our possessions can be smashed, pulverized and blown away, but I've come to realize "things" are not that important.

After the bombing, I stood on a street corner with no car, no home, and no workplace. Besides the few items in my plastic bags, I had only the clothes on my back. Even then I felt supernaturally comforted as though I were being held close in the arms of Jesus. My relationship with Him—that's what is important.

It was truly a Godsend when engineers determined the Regency could be saved. A rescue company was sent in to clean and pack everything for storage until residents became permanently relocated.

Several months later while unpacking the salvaged items, I discovered my pictures and Grandma's two beautiful quilts in perfect condition. Jubilant, I thanked God, gratefully buried my face in them and breathed in their sweet ancient fragrance. In a waterfall of tears, the memories of my wonderful childhood, and of Grandma Hattie's molding my life and teaching me to sew flooded over me. God had given me a new life—even better than the last— and I felt at home again!

*". . . while we are at home in the body*
*we are absent from the Lord . . .*
*We are confident, yes, well pleased rather*
*to be absent from the body and to be present with the Lord."*
*1 Corinthians 5:6,8*

# Wonder Woman

*as told by Ava Forrester*
*to Judy Howard*

When I called eighty-seven year old Ava Forrester, I knew I'd be lucky to catch her in.

"I just walked in the door from trimming my crepe myrtles and trees," she said. "I filled both black dumpsters to overflowing, so it's time to quit. I've got about twenty minutes before I have to leave for my weight-lifting class. What can I do for you?"

I explained to Ava that I was looking for quilt stories for my next book, stories that would tell Oklahoma's history through women and their quilts.

Ava volunteered that her mom taught her how to quilt on their farm near Wanette, Oklahoma when Ava was only five years old. Ava was already her mom's right hand, helping with the cotton, corn and peanut harvest, the big vegetable garden, and fruit orchard, as well as milking the cows, slopping the pigs and churning butter. After lightning killed their team of black mares in the 1940s, Ava's folks sold their farm and moved to Shawnee.

I asked Ava what she and her family had done for fun during the Depression, despite so much work and a fair amount of hardship.

"When I was eight and my twin sisters were ten, we sang church songs on the Shawnee radio station," she said. "And Dad loved to play dominos. When Ava's older brother turned sixteen, Dad let him drive the kids around, but only after we played dominos with him. When Ava's brother turned twenty-one, he caught pneumonia working in the oil fields and died, leaving his three-month-old baby for the grandparents to raise. "And would you believe," Ava asked, clearly still amazed, "the first thing Dad taught his grandson was to play dominos?"

Ava loved to eavesdrop on the gossip at the quilting bees held in the neighbors' homes and often shared a pot of beans with the ladies. Ava helped her mom make scrapbag and feed sack clothes and quilts to keep them warm.

"Can you believe Oklahoma Quiltworks sells feed sack material by the bolt now, sixty years later?" Ava added.

"I'm making a patriotic red and blue Lone Star quilt for my Viet Nam soldier son who's 100% disabled. He's building a new house, and this will be a surprise for his housewarming gift," Ava said, excitedly. Ever since Melba Lovelace listed Ava's name as a hand-quilter in her Melba's Swapshop column in the *Oklahoman* thirty years ago, Ava has been deluged with requests to quilt for others

I was struck not only with how busy Ava's life has been, but also with the number of truly tragic events that have happened to those she's loved best. Ava agreed. "Besides my sister's dying when she was twenty-seven," Ava said, "my husband took off when I still had an eleven-year-old boy and a thirteen-year-old girl to raise. That was in 1950. I had to support my family with no money and no education."

"What did you do?"

"I bawled so long, my eyes drooped. Then a woman named Frances knocked on my door to sell Amway and wanted to teach me how," Ava replied. After following Frances around for a day, Ava decided she could sell Amway, too. Before long, she was selling more than Frances ever thought about selling. Ava graduated from Amway to being a Fuller Brush super salesman and then selling furniture at Evans, Sneeds, and Furniture Trends. Later, she applied at Rothschilds in Penn Square to sell fur coats to make some real money. Since selling fur coats wasn't an option, Rothschilds put Ava in ready-to-wear. Ava made more the first month than the other salesman had made in the last three years she'd been with the company.

"Now I make drapes for two decorators and some wealthy families," Ava said. She probably could have told me a few more stories, but it was getting late and Ava had weight-lifting class. After that, she and her gentleman friend were going dancing. "I told him up front that I didn't want to get married or go to bed," Ava explained, "and we've been having a ball ever since. We even went on a few vacations together. We walk two miles daily and go dancing twice a week."

With so many hardships and such a great attitude, I asked Ava what her secret was.

"Eat right, exercise and trust God to look after you," she said. "And I keep busy with my quilting along with everything else. Tomorrow I begin my computer classes."

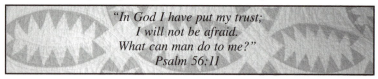

*"In God I have put my trust;*
*I will not be afraid.*
*What can man do to me?"*
*Psalm 56:11*

# Building Bridges
## of Patchwork
### by Joy Neal Kidney

I collapsed onto a stool in one corner of the delivery room as Fuada, the exhausted mother, dozed.

Hasan, her husband, took pictures of the plump naked baby on a warming table, gloating, "My son, my son. First grandson. First one before my brother."

*What did he mean? And what on earth am I doing here with these people?* I wondered.

Even as I thanked God for this beautiful perfect baby, my mind was reeling. The night before, Hasan had acted wacky, ranting that he was going to the police if the baby wasn't "100 percent."

I didn't realize then that this young father, just twenty-eight, was starting to sink into severe mental illness.

Two years earlier, as an English-as-a-Second-Language volunteer at my church, I had met Hasan's brothers—Sejad, Fehim, and Mirsad. I was surprised to learn that these haggard-looking Bosnian refugees were only in their twenties, the same age as my own son, who was in graduate school, going to ball games, and playing pool on week-ends. My heart went out to them. *Dear Lord, how can I help them? They need a lot more than English.* But I didn't seem to have any other useful skills.

I soon helped them find jobs and drove them to appointments.

One day Mirsad's daughter Larisa was home from school. "Oh, is she sick?" I asked.

"No, today Muslim holy day," her father revealed.

*Muslim! Dear God, what have I gotten into?* Having met them at my church, I'd assumed they were Baptist, at least Christian.

But God already had knit my heart to the hearts of these people. Later that day, I went with Sejad, Fehim and Mirsad to the airport to pick up the last brother Hasan, who had flown from Bosnia with his weary wife Fuada and two-year-old son Jasna.

Over the months of sharing birthdays, lamb roasts, and holidays with the four brothers and their families, I learned that their parents' homes had been destroyed during the Bosnian war. Hasan had been wounded and Fuada had lost her two older brothers.

Hasan's moods began to swing between gratefulness for my help and suspicion. I prayed for grace to serve this struggling family and for ways to demonstrate God's love to them.

An extraordinary opportunity came when Hasan announced that Fuada was going to have another baby. "Could you please go to Fuada's doctor's appointments with her? And to the hospital with us when the baby is born?"

"Of course, I would be happy to," I quickly agreed. I also wanted to give them something special and personal. God reminded me of my old hobby of quilting, and before long I'd cut out blocks for a colorful Baby Blocks quilt.

As Fuada's date grew near, her doctor suggested inducing labor. When Hasan learned about it, he raged, "The doctor is crazy! This is no normal. I want guarantee 100 percent that my son be okay."

That's when Hasan threatened to go to the police if anything went wrong.

Early the next morning, he called to make sure I'd still go with them. Arriving at their apartment, I found Hasan pacing, holding their towel-covered Qu'ran. Fuada calmly waddled to the door with her suitcase, then explained to Jasna that he would go to a relative's apartment for a few days.

As soon as we got to the hospital, Hasan began threatening the staff. He called the refugee office, and, thankfully, his case worker finally calmed him down.

Several hours later, a beautiful perfect baby boy was born, but Hasan's paranoia had made the day bittersweet. I went home exhausted. In one corner of the baby quilt, I began to stitch, "To celebrate Kenan Zovic."

When Fuada and baby Kenan went home, I took a pan of lasagna and the baby quilt to welcome them. Fuada and Jasna excitedly ran their hands over the bright patches. But Hasan's thoughts were on his brother as he exploded, "Mirsad no come for my son. I no come for his baby."

Today, Kenan is a personable brown-eyed first grader. I've gotten in on the births of his little brother and a cousin, and have made a dozen more baby quilts for my new extended family.

I can't cure the schizophrenia which devastates Hasan and his family every few months. But when I asked God to help me bless these families, He reminded me of a humble hobby from the past.

I pray these bright baby quilts, reflecting His love and light, have helped to build bridges between our cultures, one baby at a time.

*"For if there is first a willing mind, it is accepted according to what one has, and not according to what he does not have." 2 Cor. 8:12*

# Heavenly Patchwork in a Tree House

*as told by Freda Hill*
*to Judy Howard*

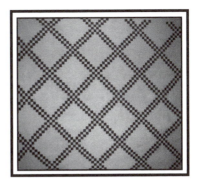

That blistering hot July afternoon of 1914 on their screened-in porch, Maude fanned her four-year-old daughter Freda. She bathed her frail body with cold compresses and gave her cool lemonade to lower the fever raging through her. "The doctor cautioned me that scarlet fever could easily develop into rheumatic fever if we didn't lower her temperature quickly," Maude told her husband. The red spots on Freda's neck had spread over her face, torso and hands. Maude felt so helpless, and exhausted after staying up with Freda three nights.

"Everything's going to be all right," her husband reassured her. "Haven't we been praying for Freda's healing? Where's that strong faith in God your mother instilled in you? I'll take the night shift so you can get some sleep." Obviously, her husband considered it a good sign that Freda's sore throat was gone.

For the next four months, Maude tenaciously nursed Freda back to health, at first mostly watching her sleep, later teaching her Bible stories, poetry and quilting. Maude wrapped Freda in a small quilt she had made as a child herself, which they now called Freda's Healing quilt because it always seemed to comfort and cheer the girl.

"Tell me the story about my Healing Quilt," Freda begged time after time.

"I was a rough and tough tomboy deluxe as a child," her mother would begin. "I did everything my brothers did, except better. I even helped them build a tree house outside the kitchen door on the family's cattle ranch near Chicago."

Maude went on telling her daughter how in 1892 when Maude was thirteen, she gathered dressmaker's scraps and cut them into two-inch squares. "What in the world are you doing cutting up that fabric?" her older brother scolded her. "Mom's going to be furious!"

"I'm making a Tree House quilt," she'd tell him. "You just try to stop me."

So every day, that summer Maude lugged fabric squares, scissors, needles and thread up the rickety board steps to the top of the tree house and stitched those tiny pieces together. Her mom helped her layer the top over batting and muslin backing and helped Maude quilt it.

"What happened to your tree house?" Freda always asked.

Maude explained how soon after, she had to leave that tree house behind, because her mom and brother were diagnosed with tuberculosis. The doctor prescribed a dryer climate, so the family sold the farm, packed their belongings and moved to Oklahoma City. Maude's dad built their summer house with wrap-around screened porches at 10th and North Walker where St. Anthony's Hospital stands today. About this point in the story, Freda always slipped into a peaceful slumber.

By her teens, under her mother's tutelage, Freda was proficient in quilt-making. Looking through a magazine one day, Maude suggested, "Let's make this Morning Glory appliquéd quilt for your hope chest. And I can make you this pretty Rose of Sharon quilt for your wedding gift, if you like."

"Oh, Mom, they're both beautiful. I can't wait," exclaimed Freda. "Can we use blues for the morning glory and yellows for the roses in that elegant soft cotton fabric that feels like silk?"

Maude agreed. So after a year of appliquéing the flowers, they completed the tops and asked the ladies of the First United Methodist Church to hand-quilt them.

As a young wife, Freda created a beautiful blue and pink sateen embroidered Nursery Rhyme quilt for her second son. Now, fifty years later, Freda's daughter-in-law Julie keeps that quilt on her bed for the four visiting grandsons to wrap up in.

"What's your secret for living a happy life?" Julie once asked her ninety-five year old mother-in-law.

"Just keep going and giving thanks," Freda confided. For Freda that meant driving her car and enjoying bridge, sewing clubs, her twice-weekly china painting classes and serving in the First Presbyterian Church Archives Department. "The Lord has blessed me with good health and a zest for living," she reminded her daughter-in-law. Freda's mother taught her to persevere with the tenacity of a bulldog. Long after Freda got over her childhood illness, her mother Maude and her mother's Tree House quilt were great inspirations to Freda.

> *"Consider it pure joy, my brothers, whenever you face trials . . ., because you know that the testing of your faith develops perseverance. Perseverance must finish its work so that you may be mature and complete, not lacking anything." James 1:2-4 NIV*

# Quilting Heals
## Biker Mama

*by Judy Howard*

Ah Maine! Antiquing along its beautiful coastline, a lifetime dream, became a reality this fall after twenty-eight years in the antique business.

"Do you have any antique quilts or any quilt stories?" I asked Hanna, who called herself the contractor woman manager of the antique mall. Husky Hanna, with her spiked hair, dainty pink crystal earrings, and tattooed bracelet had stories. I could *feel* them. "I'm a quilt dealer from Oklahoma City, and I'm writing a book of warm, fuzzy quilt stories . . . for charity."

"I don't have any quilts," Hanna said, "but I might be able to help you with a story. I used to be really fat from eating Ding Dongs, Pop Tarts and Whoopie Pies by the box load. That was in 1993 when I first got married and lost my mom in the same year. I was on a self-destructive path and knew I had to make some drastic changes.

"Instead of eating while I watched TV, I started cutting out circles and sewing little YoYos for a quilt from my mom's pretty, floral, ditsy housedresses. It was as easy and satisfying as popping candy into my mouth — a real no-brainer. I could just hear my mom shouting down from heaven, 'Hanna, you're a nut! Why don't you throw away those nasty old clothes of mine?'

"But I couldn't bear to part with any of them," Hannah continued. "They drew me closer to Mama. The housedresses still smelled of her perfume — something tangible I could hold on to. It felt like getting a big hug from her. God comforted me and cured my depression in the process of creating that YoYo quilt. I would have gone to pieces, otherwise."

Suddenly, I felt something nudge my leg. "Oh what an adorable puppy!" I said as I bent to pet her small dog.

"That's Precious, my pit bull. I rescued her from the animal shelter. My mean old ex-husband stole Prissie, my original pit bull. I was heartbroken, because the jerk wouldn't even give me visiting privileges. So Precious fills the void. She loves my Easter egg house decorated in frilly pastel pink and green fru fru, don't you, baby? Something else my ex wouldn't allow."

"Have you made any other quilts?" I asked, changing the subject.

"Oh yes. That's what I do to supplement my income all winter long when the tourist season is dead. I love to make wall-hanging quilts and pillows out of old chiffon, velvet, floral and lace curtains. Then I sell them on Ebay. Sewing is the only way to maintain my sanity with cabin fever. I'm a southern girl, a graduate of Sweetbriar Women's College in Virginia. I get so lonely I'd go nuts if it weren't for my quilting and quilting buddies. There's a sisterhood you share and immediate bond with every quilter you meet, you know?"

"I couldn't agree more," I told her and thanked her for sharing her fascinating story.

*"Sorrow and sighing, shall flee away.*
*I, even I, am He who comforts you."*
*Isaiah 51:llb-12a*

## *Martha's Passion and Compassion*

### *as told by Martha Harrisberger*

"Look what I found," Martha Harrisberger excitedly told her husband Bill as she held up a small Nine Patch doll quilt she discovered among the doll clothes she'd made as a child. "I'd forgotten I even made it." She thought of those summer days, sewing on the farm with Grandmother Winkler. The farm was the one Martha's grandfather's mother Margaret had homesteaded in the Land Run of 1889 nine miles south of Perry, Oklahoma. "Can you imagine a widow with four teenagers coming in a covered wagon to stake claim on 160 acres of barren wilderness just so her children could have a future inheritance?" Martha asked Bill, thinking that her grandmother's hardships and loneliness must have been difficult to endure.

Though Martha had sewn her own clothes since she was a child, she didn't take up quilting until she retired from school teaching and enrolled in a quilting class with her neighbor.

Suddenly, Martha's quilting became a passion—mostly for others. She recently created a Memory Quilt for Jolie Day, whose mentally challenged nine-year-old daughter Amber died in a tragic accident. Martha transferred the studio portraits of Amber onto fabric and mounted them in clouds in a blue sky with Amber's dress scraps pieced crazy quilt style for the border.

Then, Martha made a second Memory quilt for her niece Kimberly when Kimberly's nine-day-old son died. The pictures Martha appliquéd onto the clouds included Kimberly and her husband with their then newborn son, then later the family at the graveyard with the tiny white casket. Martha also included Bible verses and drawings by Kimberly's

older children. Their drawings are of Jesus welcoming the baby to heaven, angels, and a silhouette of Jesus. Kimberly's three-year-old son drew a picture of the baby with a pale face before he went to heaven and a picture of the child with a bright red face after he went to heaven. Both mothers received the quilts with joy and tears and both cherish their keepsake Memory quilts.

On a happier note, Martha recently made three Prayer quilts for cancer survivors. One was for her pastor's wife, featuring caricatures of Red Hat Ladies all in pink and purple arranged in the shape of a heart.

For a gentleman friend, Martha created the second Prayer quilt from a log cabin quilt top she'd never finished. And the third Prayer quilt she made by ripping apart a flying geese top she'd started years ago. On all three quilts, she attached ribbons. Each time Sunday school class members prayed for healing for the cancer patient, they tied the dangling ribbons into bows to remind themselves to continue praying and that they were connected by prayer to the Great Physician.

Martha was feeling sorry for the Katrina victims since her brother was himself evacuated, so she made a quilt and shipped it to the Houston International's Quilt project, "Comfort America."

It's people like Martha expressing their compassion in acts of kindness who make a difference, one quilt at a time. They do this by extending God's love and healing in small, personal ways to those who are hurting.

*"Therefore, as the elect of God, holy and beloved,*
*put on tender mercies, kindness, humility,*
*meekness, longsuffering;"*
*Colossians 3:13*

# Mamie's Masterpiece

### *by Linda McFaddin*

"I'm sorry, Mrs. Hughes, nothing less than the removal of the entire eye will halt the spread of the cancer." The doctor's voice was soft as he delivered the bad news to my mother. Thinking diversion would be helpful while we waited for the doctor to see us, I had given my mother a new quilting magazine to look at. Now she sat quietly, her fingers thumbing the edges.

Mother often said, "I'd rather quilt than eat." Like me, I know she wondered if the prognosis was the end of her sewing days.

Her interest in quilting began in her childhood as she watched her mother cut, piece, and stitch quilts to keep the family of seven warm in the Arkansas Ozarks winters. Later, in her own home, Mother made many "serviceable" quilts for her family. Whenever she could find a few minutes during the day, Mother fashioned scraps of flannel, double knit, feed sacks, and cotton prints, into her quilts. Occasionally, she selected special cotton calicos and made "fancy" quilts for one of her children or grandchildren. As the years sailed by, and her household chores waned, quilting consumed more of her time and became her favorite activity.

My stomach began churning at the doctor's words and I struggled to keep my emotions from reaching my voice and face.

Mother, on the other hand, calmly said, "I want to have the surgery as soon as possible." She took the news in stride, her usual response to challenges in life. "I'm no better than anyone else to have cancer," she later asserted to her family.

Mother recovered quickly and my phone rang one Saturday. Excitement was evident in her voice as she asked, "Can you take me to the fabric store today to buy materials for a new quilt? I found a Stained Glass pattern in a magazine you gave me, and I'm ready to get started on it."

"I'll be there right after lunch," I answered, eager to see the quilt pattern she had chosen. Later that day we purchased shiny chintz fabric in complementary colors of rose, peach, green, golden yellow, and blue, along with fabric for the blocks, backing and the "leading" part of the design.

"I'm ready to begin the quilting now," Mother wrote in a letter several months later. Soon afterward, she announced to her family, "The Stained Glass quilt is finished. Do you want to see it?" "Oohs" and "Aahs" came from everyone and Mother beamed over what she claimed was "the prettiest quilt I ever made." She had hand-stitched it by herself while adjusting to having sight in only one eye.

I persuaded Mother to enter her quilt in the Senior Division at the Tulsa State Fair. When the voice on the phone said, "Mrs. Hughes, your quilt has won a third place ribbon," Mother was all smiles. Because I had given her the magazine which inspired her to make the work of art, Mother gave the quilt to me. It hung on a wall in my home for many years, where anyone who saw the quilt admired it. Although she made numerous beautiful quilts after this one, the Stained Glass quilt was always her favorite.

Cancer never diminished my mother's spirit, but it eventually claimed her life in June 1994. Her obituary read, "Mamie Russell Hughes, quilt maker," recognition by her children of her most fulfilling work. In memory of her, many family members brought one or more of Mother's quilts to the church for her service. They were hung on quilt racks and screens in the entryway into the church and made a beautiful display. However, Mother's favorite quilt was given the place of honor and hung on the wall in the sanctuary behind the altar. With lights shining on the glistening chintz fabric, the quilt indeed looked like a stained glass window.

*"Then Jesus spoke to them again, saying, 'I am the light of the world. He who follows Me shall not walk in darkness, but have the light of life.'" John 8:12*

# Pearl's Betty Boop Quilt

### as told by Pearl Homblier to Judy Howard

One of nine children born on a farm in Arlington, Oklahoma in 1917, Pearl Hombleir worked hard all her life, but never lost her sense of humor. She created her latest whimsical quilt from *The Daily Oklahoman* newspaper photo of collector stamps showing nine Betty Boop poses. She even made a quilt for her son from cartoon characters Maggie, Jigs and Popeye.

During the nine months she sat in the hospital with her dying husband, Pearl created a quilt. The nurses loved to check her progress and asked why she was making it. Pearl quickly explained, "It's comforting to stitch and meditate on God's faithfulness and receive His peace, joy and comfort like a river flowing through my soul. Piecing these scraps together into something beautiful lifts my spirits above this hospital room into the heavenlies."

# Grandpa's Love Memorialized

### as told by Angie Cartwright to Judy Howard

David Cartwright received the devastating news of his diagnosis of cancer a week before the delivery date of his eighth grandchild. Not wanting to spoil the celebration of the new birth with his bad report, David made his wife Wanda promise not to tell anyone for a couple of months. Jokingly, he told his family on several occasions, "If something happened to me, it's not like I'm irreplaceable."

Doting on his precious new granddaughter, David dropped by on his way to and from work to hold and rock her. When he finally did announce that he would be going in for cancer surgery in three weeks, the family was crushed.

"We've got to do something to show David how special he is and that he's not replaceable," Angie Cartwright told her sister-in-law Angie Spencer. "Since the grandkids can't be with David at the hospital, let's make a quilt with the children's handprints so their love and thoughts can go with him."

So the two Angies composed a poem entitled, "A Pawpaw just for me." The poem told how Grandpa was always there for each of them when they were hurting or when they were happy. It also made it clear that they believed God had sent Grandpa to teach them about love. Then they collected a muslin block of each child's handprint with a message for Grandpa.

Nine-year-old Chandler wrote, "You're my best buddy in the world!"

Oldest grandson Josh said, "I like to go on adventures and camping with you."

"I love spending time with you," ten-year-old Turner wrote.

Angie hurriedly pieced the blocks together and took the top to Susie at Just Stitchin Quilt Shop in Cedar Hills, Texas. Susie completed the machine quilting the night before David went into the hospital—just in time for a tearful presentation before the surgery.

Luckily, David's surgery was successful and the grandkids' quilt was the perfect healing balm to remind him of his family's love and his motivation for living.

*"And this is His commandment: that we should believe on the name of His Son Jesus Christ and love one another . . ."1 John 3:23*

## In Good Hands

*by Ann McDonald*

Thirty-five years ago I saw an illustration in a magazine of a Family Hand quilt. Because my grandmother Grace Whitlow was a longtime quilter, I showed it to her. She quilted out of necessity in her early life as a farm wife with eight children to keep warm at night. My grandmother continued creating quilts as gifts for her grandchildren and for others, too, to earn a little "egg money."

Grace asked everyone in the family to send a drawing of his hands. Then she transferred the drawings onto cloth. I helped her appliqué each pair of hands onto a quilt block. Using fabric paint, Grandma embroidered the names and birthdates of each person on each block. We had a wonderful time working together on the quilt.

I asked Grandma what she was going to do with the quilt when it was finished.

She smiled with her usual good humor and said, "I want ya'll to bury me in it so I'll be in good hands!"

That story is told and the quilt is displayed each year at our family reunion. Being the oldest grandchild, I was blessed to receive the Hand quilt when Grandma died three years after completing it. My son was the youngest to have his handprint included. His children Mallori, Mason, and Madison McDonald are pictured playing on the quilt at our 2005 reunion.

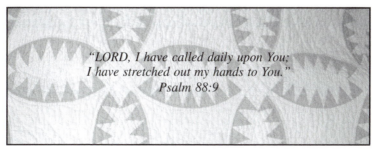

*"LORD, I have called daily upon You;*
*I have stretched out my hands to You."*
*Psalm 88:9*

# School Reunion Yields Surprise

*by Ruth Garner Boyd and Ann Garner Springer*

"We have a special surprise for you," the Bethany High School 2005 reunion chairman told me and my sister Ann as we pinned on our nametags. "Don't miss the Friendship quilt on display in the gym. It's signed by the Bethany, Oklahoma, elementary school teachers in 1934."

"Wouldn't Mom have been teaching in Bethany about then?" I excitedly asked Ann as we raced toward the gym. With anxious anticipation, we examined each signature on the red and white quilt in pristeen condition.

"Here's Mom's name in the corner," Ann exclaimed, as she wiped a tear from her eye. "It's signed 'Jewel Mae Stewart, born July 2, 1900.'"

"I'd recognize her lovely cursive handwriting any day," I said. "Today's her birthday. Do you realize she'd be 105 if she were still alive?" Pleasant childhood memories of Mom welcoming us home with fresh baked brownies flooded my soul.

The quilt's owner was introduced at the banquet that night. We praised her for preserving and protecting her historic heirloom. We also thanked the reunion committee for honoring our mom and the other teachers by displaying the legacy quilt.

We left the reunion, happy to have renewed old acquaintances and thrilled to have seen the familiar name of our loving mother preserved in a quilt we didn't know existed. Some might consider it a coincidence. But we knew it was God working anonymously to touch us with His love.

> *". . . but these are written that you may believe that Jesus is the Christ, the Son of God, and that believing you may have life in His name." John 20:31*

## Stitched in Love Especially for You
*as told by Connie Heffron to Judy Howard*

Connie had came to know that God loved and forgave her no matter what she had done in the past. But every holiday and especially on the boy's birthday, Connie's loving husband Jack watched as Connie shed tears over the son she never knew.

It was a private adoption when Connie was only sixteen, but she had signed papers promising not to ever contact the adoptive parents.

Jack researched adoption records and surprised Connie one day with the name and address of her grown son Kevin. Excited with the prospects of meeting Kevin, Connie joined the local Adoption Support Group for help in dealing with her anxiety.

"But what if he hates me for deserting him as a baby?" Connie tearfully asked Julie, the Adoption Support Group President. "I couldn't live with the pain of his rejection if he said he couldn't forgive me."

"What if I telephoned Kevin to see if he'd like to talk to you?" Julie offered.

"Oh, could you? I can't make the call myself. That would be wonderful," Connie replied hopefully.

The next morning, Julie phoned Connie with good news. Kevin wanted to speak with her. Connie immediately called Kevin and visited with this long-lost son, exchanging information and starting to get acquainted with him.

"Do you have red hair?" he asked. "My first born son has dark red hair and I've always wondered where it came from."

With a chuckle, Connie admitted that her mom, Kevin's grandmother, had red hair. When Kevin said he'd like to meet Connie in person, Connie quickly asked, "How about tomorrow?" After consulting his wife, Kevin invited his new mom to come up for a visit. So, after a sleepless night, Connie and Jack left early Saturday morning for Kansas.

Connie and Jack had a delightful time getting to know their new son, daughter-in-law and three grandchildren. Then Connie took Kevin aside and explained her actions as a young teenager living, unsupervised, with her divorced father. "I was lonely and sought love and companionship in all the wrong places. I was heartbroken over my decision to give you up for adoption, but I only wanted what was best for you. Desperately, I hoped to meet you someday, and hoped that you would accept me," she sobbed.

"After you came of age, I decided to take the risk of finding you again, even if it meant rejection," Connie admitted. "I had to tell you how much I loved you and that it broke my heart to give you up. But I was too young, poor and alone to care for you properly." Then Connie asked Kevin for forgiveness.

"Oh, Connie, I totally understand and forgive you," Kevin said, offering her a tissue. "My adoptive parents couldn't have been a better match or more loving and devoted. I had a wonderful childhood and don't blame you for anything. You acted in my best interest. That's the main thing."

A month later, Kevin and his family came to Connie's home and spent the weekend, meeting the rest of the family and building lasting relationships. Kevin looks much like Connie's three other sons and daughter and shares common hobbies like racing cars and riding motorcycles. Kevin and Connie talk monthly and now enjoy a big family reunion every year.

Carrying on the tradition of her great-grandmother, Connie has made quilts for each of her children and grandchildren. For her daughter living in Texas, Connie created a Road to Oklahoma quilt. For Jay, her oldest son who's a minister, Connie quilted a Jacob's Ladder. For Mark, her youngest son who is a youth minister, she made a King's Crown. To Kenneth who likes to build race cars, Connie gave a quilt with a big Ford emblem appliquéd in the middle with checkered flag borders.

Last Christmas, Connie presented Kevin with a symbol of home and her undying love in her beautiful hand-made Log Cabin quilt. The label attached to the back expresses her sentiments, "Stitched with Love and Made Especially for You, Mom." Connie explained to Kevin how important family is to her. "I'm leaving part of me behind with you in this quilt to wrap you with my hugs."

*"Can a woman forget her nursing child, and not have compassion on the son of her womb? Surely they may forget, Yet I will not forget you. See, I have inscribed you on the palms of My hands;"*
*Isaiah 49:15-16a*

## Giving Thanks in All Things

*by Suzanne Kistler*

Standing in line to register for Bible study at church, my ears pricked up hearing the words quilt group. "Excuse me," I said, tapping the curly grey-haired lady on the shoulder, "did you say something about a guild?"

She smiled and nodded. "Oh, yes. My guild. I love my guild. It's the Valley Oak Quilt Guild."

"Your guild? I thought that was my guild. I'm Suzie Kistler. Who are you?"

"Well, I'm Mary Hoffman."

*Mary Hoffman*. I'd heard that name before. In fact, I'd been praying for her healing since I'd begun attending this church. She didn't look like she was suffering, but I'd heard the prayer requests many times.

We immediately became friends, our friendship cemented by our common bond.

It wasn't long before she stopped attending Bible study. Trying to concentrate on Isaiah was too much when undergoing weekly doses of chemo. Instead, she concentrated on color, design and friendships.

When my mother passed away, even though Mary was still going through her own health crisis, she gave me hugs and comfort. She reassured me that God is in control, He knows what's best, He doesn't make mistakes, and that Jesus is coming soon to take us home. Mary wept with me, yet helped me see the hope.

I watched Mary and learned from her. While Mother feared her cancer, Mary considered cancer a blessing. She often said things could be worse, and she praised the Lord for giving her the gift of quilting. Quilting was a source of peace and comfort when much of her life was beyond her control.

Talk about "Joy in the Lord." Mary had that down pat. As cancer took more and more of her active life away, Mary's joy radiated even more. She invited friends to visit and we were blessed by her words and her prayers. Greeting everyone with a smile, Mary gave thanks for all things, and sent us each off with a prayer.

The last time I saw Mary, she told me she wouldn't be here much longer. She wasn't worried about herself because she knew exactly where she was headed.

"Please tell the quilters what a blessing and encouragement they've been to me. Don't think that just because I'm gone I'll stop praying for ya'll."

Mary's enthusiasm was priceless. The following week at her memorial service, my sentiments about Mary were echoed by others. The Worship Director grinned and shook his head as he told us what songs we were about to sing. "Mary personally picked out these rip-roaring, foot-stomping praise songs."

As we belted out "When we all get to heaven, what a day of rejoicing that will be," I thought about Mary. Mary Hoffman was a treasure — a quilter whose life blessed mine and countless others because of her faith and obvious joy in the Lord.

*"Rejoice always, pray without ceasing, in everything give thanks; for this is the will of God in Christ Jesus for you." 1 Thess5:16-8*

# Forgotten Farms

*from Lois Lyon's note attached to the quilt she gave her mom for Christmas in 2002*

Merry Christmas, Mom. Does this Forgotten Farms quilt bring back fond memories of the crazy trip we took in 1983 to the National Quilt Association show in Bellbuckle, Tennessee? I thought we'd never get home stopping to take hundreds of pictures of old barns along the country roads to inspire me to create this quilt.

Each block was like painting a picture and reliving our trip. My sweet friend Marilyn Karper loved quilting it by machine. She used a different pattern for the clouds, grasses and grounds and quilted around each tree and bush. She even embellished the barns with her stitching to make the boards look realistic. I bordered the quilt with faux wood fabric to complete the rustic look.

I've included Nancy Davis-Merty's narrative telling the location and story behind each barn. Do you recognize my favorite—the famous round barn on Route 66 in Arcadia, Oklahoma? Barn dances were held to raise money to construct it in 1898 and it's still standing strong today as one of Oklahoma's icons. The construction workers refused to sleep in the seemingly unstable structure. It certainly fooled the skeptics didn't it?          Love, Lois

*Be my strong refuge,*
*To which I may resort continually;*
*You have given the commandment to save me,*
*For You are my rock and my fortress.*
*Psalm 71:3*

*Memorial Quilts*

# The Most Thoughtful Gift
### by Molly Lemmons

"All it takes for a man to be happy is a good wife and a good pair of overalls."

These words of our father to us five children when we were small were what he earnestly believed. A building contractor in the Oklahoma City area for almost thirty years, Daddy literally *lived* in his overalls.

"Now, Morris Rogers," Mother would say, "You wear those overalls *everywhere*, but you mustn't wear them to church!"

Daddy grinned. Such a thought surely never crossed his mind as he "twinkled" in the light of Mother's knowing smile. I don't remember Daddy's ever leaving for work nor coming home that he wasn't whistling.

"Morris, you act like you own the world," Mother commented one day as he came in whistling.

"*My Father does*," was his reply.

One night, Mother called us to come into the living room. "I have an announcement to make," she told us. We seated ourselves around her, my sister Sally Ann age thirteen, me, age eleven, and brother Bob, age seven, eagerly awaiting Mother's news. "I'm *that way*," she said quietly. (Mother never would say the word *'pregnant.'*)

"May I tell Daddy?" I asked excitedly.

"I think your father knows it."

Six months later, our sister Polly Pat was born and Daddy even wore his overalls to the hospital.

Three years later, Mother again announced she was "that way" and our baby sister Ellen Sue was born six months afterwards. And you guessed it—Daddy wore his overalls to the hospital that night, too.

When Mother died in 1997, Daddy felt deserted without his mate of sixty-four years. He found his main comfort in his beautiful garden. My favorite memory is Daddy in his overalls and hat in his garden, leaning on his hoe and wiping his brow with his shirtsleeve. He always said that being in the garden was his time with the Lord.

Not long after Mother's death, Daddy fell and fractured his back. His eyesight almost completely gone, he opted to sell the house that he had built for Mother when he retired in 1968. He then entered an assisted living facility. Daddy didn't want to be a burden to his children.

Daddy loved to eat peanut butter straight from the jar. Sometimes he didn't see well enough to keep it off the bib of his overalls. "Aw, Molly Lou," he'd say sheepishly to me, "would you *look* at *that*? I can't seem to hit my mouth!" And he'd wipe "at" the spot on the front of his overalls, chuckling all the while.

The night Daddy died in 2002 and we had said our goodbyes to the dearest father on earth, I left the residence without going back to his room. I knew that Polly Pat would tend to cleaning the room out and disposing of his overalls and shirts … *I thought!*

The following Christmas, Polly Pat said she had a surprise for her four siblings. We gathered at Ellen Sue's house and Polly Pat passed out the packages. I opened mine first. There before me was the most thoughtful gift I could ever receive.

I held in my hands a quilt made from Daddy's overalls. Polly Pat had made five quilts, one for each of us. My quilt had the "bib," complete with peanut butter stains. My quilt also had the pocket in which Daddy kept his Bible that he wanted always with him. As a girl, when I asked him why, he said, "to be ready always to give an answer to every man that asketh you a reason of the hope that is in you …" (I Peter 3:15)

As I lifted the quilt from its box, intermingled tears of sorrow, loneliness, joy, and *healing* poured onto my cheeks and spilled onto my sweater. Memories of Daddy swelled within my heart and soul. From deep within, I could hear him say: "All it takes for a man to be happy is a good wife and a good pair of overalls."

Daddy had them both. And now I had the overalls!

> *"For as many as are led by the Spirit of God, these are sons of God. For you did not receive the spirit of bondage again to fear, but you received the Spirit of adoption by whom we cry out, 'Abba, Father.' The Spirit Himself bears witness with our spirit that we are children of God, and if children, then heirs—heirs of God and joint heirs with Christ" Romans 8:14-16a*

# Twisted

### by Leslie Graham

One rainy day, my granddaughter Nicole came to visit. We were looking at quilts and Nicole was fascinated by the Oklahoma City bombing memorial quilt I'd made in 1995.

"Grandma, tell me the story about this quilt," she begged.

So I told her. Nicole was just a baby when the Alfred P. Murrah Building was bombed. I remember thanking God that Nicole was safe that day as I prayed for the people in that building. I wanted to make a quilt memorializing the building and the 168 people, including nineteen babies, whose lives were wrenched from this world.

Nicole pondered how anyone could kill and especially kill babies. Then she asked me to explain the tree I'd made as the central piece of the quilt. The tree is called the survivor tree, symbolizing God's miracle of healing and strength. "Even though the tree was burned, split and singed by the bomb, the leaves budded out the following spring, giving hope to the world that life is possible after tragedy," I explained. I showed Nicole how I'd put bloodstone beads at the trunk because it sprang up out of the blacktop. I showed her the Austrian crystal beads and explained that they represented the singed bark gouges in the tree.

"You have more beads here," Nicole observed.

So I told her that the clear crystal beads represent our tears and the rain that fell during the rescue days when the search dogs were sent into the building to find the missing. The dogs came out with bloody paws and looked depressed when they couldn't find anyone alive.

Nicole seemed to understand as she shifted her attention to something more uplifting. "What's this?" she asked, "and this?" She pointed to squares that looked like presents, flowers, crosses, teddy bears and hearts.

I explained how I'd tried to represent the chain link memorial fence with the mementos of comfort, love and encouragement that well-wishers had brought. I told my granddaughter how her grandpa and I went down to Oklahoma City to take pictures so I'd know what to include in the quilt. I showed her how I'd used silver threads in a sound waves design.

"How'd you think of the name for this quilt?" Nicole asked.

I explained that I called that quilt "Twisted" because the building, perpetrator, bodies, toys and even the trial were twisted. I carefully packed the quilt back into the trunk where it had pretty much sat since I made it. Nicole had a better idea.

"Grandma, shouldn't we keep it out and show everyone? Then they can remember the pain that one evil deed caused and never let it happen again?"

Since that day, the quilt rests on the back of my sofa. When I show people who have not yet seen it, I think of the good one person can do—of one young woman, in particular, my granddaughter, Nicole.

*"In that day, the LORD with His severe sword, great and strong, will punish Leviathan . . . that twisted serpent;"*
*Isaiah 27:1*

## America the Beautiful
### by Lena Hambrick Frost

In 1962 in Tuscaloosa, Alabama, Professor of American History John Pancake left his home in a quiet neighborhood after midnight to drive to his office. He heard a car start up the hill as he got about a block away. Turning right toward the campus then left, right, right and left again, the car followed as the professor parked outside his university office.

The racial tension at the University of Alabama had been electric since two black students had been admitted. Professor Pancake boldly got out and approached the other car, asking the two young black men inside, "Who are you? And why are you following me?"

"We're the Deacons of Defense . . . here to protect you if you encounter trouble," explained the two students from Stillman, an all-black Presbyterian College.

In 1978, my family moved next door to the Pancakes. John's wife Frances, weakened by chemotherapy, told me incredible stories of the past. "One morning during the Vietnam War, I watched on a nationally-televised newscast as our college-aged son placed a flower in the barrel of a gun at an anti-war demonstration in Washington, DC." Unafraid of controversy, the Pancakes worked diligently in the nation's Civil Rights movement.

The family's convictions regarding integration inspired them to join others in forming a new church, University Presbyterian Church, to welcome any who wanted to worship. After Frances died, the church used memorial gifts to purchase a communion set. But when John died, monetary donations were given to the university to establish the John S. Pancake Seminar Room.

In 1992, I was brainstorming with our new minister at University Presbyterian about how to brighten our dark, drab sanctuary. Knowing my passion for quilting, the minister asked me to consider creating a quilted table runner for the communion table to add some life and color.

I hesitated, but replied, "You know, the church does need some tangible memorial to commemorate the life of our founder John Pancake. Maybe I could appliqué a wreath of grapes in the center with a cross and crown on either side to cover the table top."

Later as I appliquéd those purple grapes, I prayed and thought a lot about John. *How could I remind future generations the principles this church was founded upon?* Remembering that we sang "America, the Beautiful" at John's funeral, I decided that hymn could be represented in panels that would hang over each end of the table. I excitedly began looking for just the right fabrics for the "spacious skies," the "purple mountain majesties" and the "fruited plain." The "amber waves of grain" were embroidered on top as three stalks of wheat.

Finally a date was set for the Homecoming festivities and the dedication of the table runner. John Pancake, Jr. and his wife Pam attended. It was a weekend of renewing friendships and getting acquainted with Pam, a professional harpist, who also had worked with cloth, designing a banner for her church.

The church also renewed its allegiance to America the Beautiful, one nation under God made great by trusting in our Almighty Creator who provides liberty and justice for all.

*"Some nations boast of armies and of weaponry,*
*but our boast is in the Lord our God.*
*Those nations will collapse and perish;*
*we will arise to stand firm and sure!"*
*Psalm 20:7-8 The Living Bible*

# A Time of Gifts

*by Ann McDermott*

In September of 2001, grief and pain overwhelmed me following the horrific events at the World Trade Center. I was strangled with the sense of being violated by an evil deed just as in the Oklahoma City Murrah Bombing on April 19th, 1995. The people of this community had united in helping to heal the broken and I knew this also would happen in New York City.

Stephen Jay Gould expressed this sentiment in an article written for the *New York Times.* He wrote, "The tragedy of human history lies in the enormous potential for destruction in rare acts of evil, not in the high frequency of evil people. Thus, in what I like to call the Great Asymmetry, every spectacular incident of evil will be balanced by 10,000 acts of kindness, too often unnoted and invisible as the 'ordinary' efforts of a vast majority."

After reading this, I was inspired to express this idea in a quilt. The evil is represented by the large black square in the center. The multi-colored triangles flying outward represent the 10,000 acts of kindness.

This quilt became part of an exhibit titled, "America: From the Heart." Within six weeks after the terrorist attacks, 270 quilts were created and displayed at the Houston International Quilt Festival in November 2001. The response to the exhibit was so overwhelming, that one hundred quilts were selected for a traveling exhibit. I was pleased when my wall hanging was chosen to travel around the country and to Barcelona, Spain to bring hope and comfort to the brokenhearted.

*"Therefore, as the elect of God, holy and beloved, put on tender mercies, kindness, humility, meekness, longsuffering; bearing with one another, and forgiving one another... "*
*Colossians 3:12-13*

# Celestial Send Off

*as told by Martha Green*
*to Judy Howard*

On September 11th, 2001 I flipped on CNN to catch the news and relish my last cup of morning tea. Instantly I witnessed a building explode and flames shoot out . . . Oh no! We're at war! I thought. "It appears that a second plane has just hit the World Trade Center," the reporter speculated.

The scars were still tender from Oklahoma City's own Alfred P. Murrah Building bombing.

How can our nation survive another disaster, I wondered and immediately began to pray. God help us!

As I watched the tragedy unfold, I prayed for wise leadership and comfort for the families of the dead and missing. And I kept thinking, I've got to do something to bring order out of this chaos, anything to create something beautiful in the face of this horror.

So I pulled out the nine black crazy patch blocks I'd just finished piecing and began embellishing each different piece of velvet and satin with roses, daisies and hen scratch embroidery stitching. My thoughts, prayers and emotions were mapped with ribbons, beads and thread as I labored to record my healing journey—a fabric poetry of circumstance.

As I sewed, I remembered my grandmother's teaching me to piece when I was three. I thought how Grandma's family of fourteen was so poor they couldn't afford a horse to travel to Tahlequah to claim their allotted land made available in 1898 by the Dawes Commission to those on the Cherokee rolls.

Then my stitching transported me back in time to the rock concerts I attended in the early 1970s. I wore the same long denim skirt to each concert. As I sat cross-legged in the grass swaying with the rhythm of this band or that band, I embroidered the pockets and finally the bottom of the skirt. That skirt held too many memories to toss, so years later I took it apart and made my first Crazy quilt. I backed the quilt with denim and still use it for my picnic blanket. The blanket is so heavy it'll crush any tumbleweed. Seeing that skirt transformed began the passion I've had ever since with Crazy quilts.

I was thrilled when Nancy Kirk of the Quilt Heritage Foundation asked to include my work in their traveling "Spirit of America" exhibit. Over the next six months following the collapse of the twin towers, the only thing that made any sense to me was my quilting. I stitched and prayed and unconsciously memorialized the loss of lives in the tragic event. I'm still angry and sad. But I was glad that my quilt titled "Celestial Send Off" displayed around America brought a little hope and beauty to a grieving and confused nation.

> *"To comfort all who mourn, ...*
> *To give them beauty for ashes,*
> *the oil of joy for mourning,*
> *the garment of praise for the spirit of heaviness;"*
> *Isaiah 61:2-3*

## Ford V-8 Can't Outrun Stork

### by Blanche Barrymore

When I was growing up in Western Oklahoma, quilting was a social event to create a lasting gift to honor someone special. In 1943, my mother Mae Fowler organized her thirty neighbors to pay tribute to her heroic sister Ollie Cantrell, who courageously overcame the loss of three husbands and then struggled to support her three children through the Great Depression.

When Ollie died, Mom and I discovered Ollie's cherished Star Friendship quilt, carefully preserved, among her meager possessions at the nursing home. "This quilt triggers a lifetime of memories of each of these thirty dear friends and relatives," Mom told me. "Look at Peggy Joyce and Patsy Loyce's blocks. Do you remember that crazy night they were born?"

"I sure do," I said. "Only by the grace of God did the three of you survive." Mom's water broke about 9 p.m. Frightened and panicky, Dad grabbed a quilt for warmth since their car had no heater. Only eight miles into the twenty mile trip to the Erick, Oklahoma hospital, Peggy Joyce popped out. Daddy attempted to tie the cord, and he wrapped her in the quilt when Mother startled him by yelling, "There's another baby coming." It shocked both of them.

In the middle of the drama, Dad stopped at a relative's house for help. Fortunately, the lady of the house was a midwife who immediately tied Peggy Joyce's cord correctly. Another relative grabbed a second quilt and hurriedly got into the back seat of the car, holding the first baby for a continued trip to the hospital.

A few miles further down the road Patsy Loyce pushed her way into the fun and mayhem. Mom immediately wrapped Patsy in the other quilt for the remaining journey to Erick. Since Peggy Joyce had arrived in Roger Mills County and Patsy Loyce was born in Beckham County, the nurse suggested they name the twins Millie and Becky for their place of origin. But Mother gave me the privilege of naming the babies.

Their births made headline news on the front page of *The Daily Oklahoman: The Ford V-8 is a fast car, but not fast enough to beat the stork.*

"Remember the times the twins made news in other ways like painting the bedroom wall with my lipstick and throwing my sandals down the outdoor toilet?" I asked Mom.

None of us could forget their mischievous trouble-making. Fortunately the twins grew to become lovely young women. And each became an expert seamstress who loved collecting fine quilts. Could the strong attraction be because they made their debut wrapped in handmade quilts that cold chaotic November eve?

*"The fear of the LORD is the instruction of wisdom, and before honor is humility."*
*Proverbs 15:33*

# The Bob Wills Quilt

*by Lawrence (Larry) D. Fisher,*
*grandson of Frances Fisher*

"Deep within my heart lies a melody," Tommy Duncan crooned the Bob Wills song *San Antonio Rose* over KVOO, 1140 on the a.m. dial from the Philtower building in downtown Tulsa, Oklahoma, on a Wednesday night in 1936. *I never tire of hearing that song,* thought Frances Fisher, a pioneer woman who came to Oklahoma before statehood in a covered wagon. Now a widow, Frances lived with her four grown children in mill row housing in Sand Springs, Oklahoma, ten miles west of downtown Tulsa and Cain's Ballroom where Bob Wills and his Texas Playboys played Saturday noon at the old-timer fiddlers contest.

"Mama, why do you want to go see Bob Wills play?" younger daughter Kathlyn, Kat to family members, was confused. "You don't dance!"

"I don't need to dance to enjoy the music. We can take the street car to Tulsa. I want to meet Bob Wills."

In those days, many commodities were packaged in unbleached printed muslin sacks made at Commander Mills, the local cotton mill, where the Fishers worked. Women used those sacks to make clothing. For months, Frances, had been collecting the front panel of Play Boy Flour sacks, saving the picture of the cowboy on a rearing horse twirling his lasso just like Will Rogers. She had a plan for those sixteen feed sack panels— she was going to make a special quilt.

Saturday morning, Frances boarded the electric trolley that traveled the loop between Sand Springs and Tulsa. Kat settled beside her in the third bench seat behind the driver. Off they went to Cain's at 423 N. Main, downtown Tulsa, with stops first at Lake Station, Twin Cities, and other points in between. She carried two bags. One contained two dozen pork chops. Frances had prepared the chops using Tommy Duncan's favorite recipe as printed in Sunday's *Tulsa World*. The other bag contained the sixteen Play Boy flour panels for her special quilt.

"Mama, what's in those bags? They smell good!" Kat tried to open the larger bag.

Frances lightly slapped Kat's fingers. "Nothing for you. It's a surprise. Just get me there early like you said you would."

They were almost an hour early. "What if I missed him? What if he's already inside? No. His bus isn't here yet." She and Kat kept watching Main Street for the red and white bus with "Bob Wills and his Texas Playboys" printed on the side above the windows.

"Here it comes." She watched the bus glide into the alley. As band members began to unload their instruments, she saw her opportunity.

"Tommy Duncan. I made your favorite recipe—pork chops, corn, and Play Boy bread crumbs layered in the pan." Tommy and the band members rushed up. "Home cookin', fellas. Thanks, lady." Her bag vanished among the band members as they passed through the back door to Cain's.

"Bob . . . Bob, could I ask a favor of you?"

Bob Wills stopped and looked at the lady in the print dress, graying hair in a bun, wire-frame glasses down on her nose.

"Bob, I've been saving Play Boy Flour feed sack panels to make a quilt. Could you and your band members each sign a panel so I could embroidery your names onto the panels and sew them together?"

Bob looked at the panel Frances was holding up. He smiled. "What's your name, lady?"

"Frances Fisher. I don't go to dances, usually. Not since my husband died last year. I just listen on the radio. I really want to make this quilt and I can't without your signatures."

*Heavenly Patchwork II---146*

"Really? Well, Mrs. Fisher, get your feed sack panels out." Bob signed a panel. He took her through the back door onto the stage. "Boys, each of you sign a cowboy here for Mrs. Fisher. She wants to make a quilt out of 'em."

Grandma couldn't believe what was happening. She was on stage with Bob Wills and the Texas Playboys! "Lady, stand right here," Bob said.

"Let's start this party." Bob picked up his fiddle and led the band in *Take Me Back to Tulsa*. Bob took her on stage in front of the band amid the applause of his fans. "Folks. Before we start this fiddler's contest, we have a special guest. Mrs. Fisher here says she's never been to one of our radio programs. Well, she's here today and she's dancing the first dance with me. Take it away, Leon."

Leon McAuliffe, steel guitar player, led *Faded Love* while Frances Ellen (Roark) Fisher danced the first refrain with Bob Wills. He then escorted her to the table where Kat watched in awe as he pulled out her chair and helped her take a seat. "You folks have a good time, ya hear?"

And they did!

She finished the Bob Wills quilt later that year and went back to Cain's to show the quilt to Bob and the band. In 1939, she entered the quilt in the Tulsa state fair where it won a cash prize.

Frances listened to BobWills music up until she died in 1980 at the age of 102. The Bob Wills quilt remained in the family until son Chester donated it to the Sand Springs museum for public viewing.

*"Yes, I will sing aloud of Your mercy in the morning;*
*for You have been my defense and refuge in the day of my trouble."*
*Psalm 16:15*

# Changing the World - One Quilt at a Time

### by Judy Howard

As a lark, I enrolled with two friends in a quilt class in the late 1970s. The class was taught by internationally known quilt artist Terrie Mangat. We met in Terrie's historic old house near downtown Oklahoma City, the place she called home while her African-born husband attended OU Medical School. Terrie taught us silk screening, block printing, and reverse appliqué. But she taught us something more: to stretch our imaginations beyond traditional quilting.

Terrie's house was bursting with bright patches of beauty, art and color. Quilt murals covered every wall. On sensory overload, we dug through Terrie's cupboards, baskets, trunks, and even an old baby bed. Each overflowed with fabric scraps, sorted by color. We marveled at Terrie's recently completed African-inspired work with rows of giraffes in reverse appliqué marching across the quilt as if heading toward their watering hole.

"What will you do with these cut-out buffalos, Indians and cowboys?" I asked, fingering the white muslin.

"Oh, those will be appliquéd in rows as the clouds on the blue sky for the *Oklahoma Quilt* the government commissioned me to make to dedicate the Murrah Federal Building." Terrie lay a few Indians along a pretty blue rim to give us the idea. "I've got to get that finished before the ribbon cutting next spring," Terrie said, as she held up the sketch showing how Oklahomans made their living off the land. "In the foreground, I'll sew rows of reverse appliquéd oil derricks, windmills, wheat and cattle. What do you think?"

"Awesome!" I exclaimed. "How do you come up with such off-the-wall ideas?"

"That's the sense of fun, adventure and artist in me," Terrie admitted proudly. She admitted that she loved to make a political statement that shocked people into re-evaluating their beliefs."

Within a year, quilting won over my heart and hands. I opened my own quilt store and began the quilt phase of my life in earnest.

Twenty-seven years later after moving my Buckboard Quilt shop home, I wrote *Heavenly Patchwork—Quilt Stories Stitched with Love*. I'm pleased that all profits go to charity quilting. While gathering Murrah Memorial quilts to display to commemorate the tenth anniversary of the bombing at my book signings, I thought of

Terrie. I called her and asked if she'd loan me her *Children's Murrah Memorial Quilt* that toured the country in the "Sewing Comfort out of Grief" exhibit. Terrie graciously consented and shipped her awe-inspiring quilt to me from her new studio in Taos.

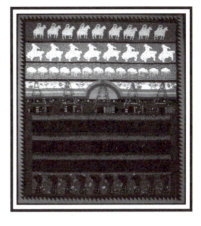

I had seen photos of the quilt. But when I unfolded this 8' x 12' quilt, valued at $10,000, I was startled to see a huge map of the United States outlined in what looked like dripping blood. The quilt was titled "By Violence." I called Terrie, anxious to learn the further story, "I see you're still shaking people out of their complacency with your shocking art. What's this all about?"

"Oh, that's my cry for help for the children killed by violence. In 1995 when the Helias Foundation asked me to make this *Children's Murrah Memorial Quilt*, I was working with children in the inner city of Louisville. You wouldn't believe the tragic tales of abuse and violence I heard," Terrie explained. She called the FBI and received an eighteen page report giving the statistics of crimes against children. Twenty-five hundred children under twelve were killed in that year alone.

"Being a political activist, I pieced together the map and appliquéd one thousand little caskets in blue and pink pinpointing where each child was killed," Terrie explained. "Then I outlined the map in red paint to look like dripping blood, and in the bottom corner I wrote the statistics about the children who were murdered." Terrie had arranged caskets in a heart shape and set these over the state of Oklahoma to symbolize the nineteen children killed in the Murrah bombing.

"You never were bashful about stating your opinion and making waves," I told her. "Love your attention to detail with the appropriate calicos used for each state." I was seeing new things now over her wonderful fabric art. "How did you come up with Elvis fabric for Tennessee?" I asked, noting her race cars for Indiana, dairy cows for Wisconsin, quarter horses for Kentucky, cowboys for Texas, red hot chilies for New Mexico, playing cards for Nevada, and sunflowers for Kansas. "You must have visited every fabric store in America to come up with specific images."

"No. Actually, I just dug through my collection of scraps and found most of them. You know what a fabric freak I am."

I well remembered her stash of fabrics in her Oklahoma City studio. I believed Terrie's *Oklahoma Quilt* and *Children's Murrah Memorial Quilt,* titled "By Violence," would go down in history as documenting the beginning and end of the Murrah Building.

As Terrie talked on, I was relieved to learn that her *Oklahoma Quilt* was rescued from hanging in the Federal Building and placed in the safety of the Archives for posterity.

Responding to my questions about her new fabric line and her latest project, Terrie replied, "Everyone loves the new line of African-inspired nature prints . . . . My latest project is the devastation from Hurricane Katrina. I had to spring into action to mobilize the quilters across the country to hold a National Quiltathon to make quilts for the victims."

As Terrie excitedly unveiled her plans, she convinced me to help in the effort to provide comforting quilts to those most in need of the touch of God's love and hope that quilts represent. As I thanked Terrie again for lending me her sensational quilt, it occurred to me that she was still doing what she'd done for me years ago. She was teaching people to stretch their imaginations to fit their lives. In good times and in bad, here was one woman sending out comfort, one quilt at a time.

*"So the ransomed of the LORD . . .*
*shall obtain joy and gladness;*
*sorrow and sighing shall flee away. '*
*I, even I, am He who comforts you.*
*Who are you that you should be afraid . . . ?'"*
*Isaiah 51:11-12*

*Heavenly Patchwork II---150*

# Murrah!

*by Alice Doughty Kellogg*

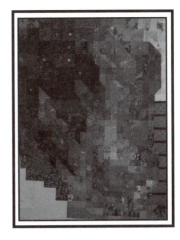

On April 19, 1995, sitting at my kitchen table reading the paper, I felt a tremor in the floor and heard two booms. My beagle Cookie cocked her head and raced to the backdoor. *On no! What's going on? Is this an earthquake? Or did one of the AWAC planes crash at Tinker?* I ran outside to check for smoke. No smoke. No sirens. I flipped on the TV. Within minutes, aerial photos revealed only the skeleton of the Murrah Federal Building in downtown Oklahoma City. What an interesting mix of white paper floating down and black smoke billowing up, I thought.

Panic gripped my heart as I remembered my husband was working less than two miles from that area. My brother worked three blocks south of the court house and a sister-in-law two blocks southeast. I called my husband and found him immediately, much to my relief. Soon the others checked in.

I sat glued to the TV the rest of the day. Volunteers pulled bloody bodies of dead or badly injured babies and adults from the Murrah Building, the YMCA, the Hightower Apartments, and the Journal Record Building nearby.

Those images remain. The assault on our peace-loving community was an outrage and robbed us of our sense of security. Two weeks after the blast, I considered making an art quilt, but the wounds were too fresh for me to be creative. I made a sketch of how I remembered the flames coming from even the nearby burning cars. Months later, I drew a mosaic of flames and started collecting fabrics to recreate the illusion of fire and smoke. I also collected appropriate novelty pictorial fabrics.

Emotionally drained, I often had to walk away from my Murrah Memorial quilt and work on something else for several weeks before my heartache subsided and let me return to the troubled fabric landscape. I redesigned the quilt twice because my husband accidentally kept knocking the pieces off my design wall and I couldn't remember where the pieces fit.

God brought comfort from my grief and anger, and calmness out of chaos in the process of my piecing those one-inch squares together.

*151---Memorial*

The finished quilt is a giant flame with smoke, ash and debris billowing out of the Murrah Building. On closer inspection, viewers spot the "fussy-cut" novelty fabrics, like the car with the happy family in front of the building, obviously unaware of the danger. I included a skull-and-crossbones, toys, Tweety Bird with a look of surprise in his big blue eyes, and a helicopter in the sky. I sewed buttons onto the black and gray fabrics to make them shimmer like the ash and paper that fluttered in the sunlight of that day.

My memorial quilt hung in the 1997 Central Oklahoma Quilt Show and people often commented on its bold colors. But when they read the title "Murrah!" they grew silent and looked closer at the novelty prints before moving on to the other nearby quilts.

Many people talk about the healing process and "closure." But I never will heal completely from that senseless act of violence against innocent people, especially the children. The anger that I felt that day lingers on and I find I don't really want to let it go.

*"I, even I, am He who comforts you." Isaiah 51:12a*

## The Children

*by Nancy Barrett*

That April morning began like the others before it, sunny, new flower faces, the chipper songs of birds and hope. But at the close of day, my whole world had changed. Forever. I was grumpily ripping out a seam on a quilt I'd been making (never my favorite task) when I heard the *Ka-Boom . . . Boom*. The windows rattled. Something horrible had happened. I only could pray for those who might have been injured or killed and wait for news. A call from my frantic mother was the first inkling that something was indeed very, very wrong. Quickly I thought where my husband Don was off to that day and realized he was safe. But many were not. As the hours and early weeks unfolded after the Murrah bombing, the stories were so poignant, painful, and even miraculous.

As we learned more and more about our "home grown" terrorist, we mourned the loss of our sense of safety and grieved the loss of friends and family members. One of my quilting students had been killed. She'd just begun quilting, but felt she was getting the knack of it and was excited and full of plans for other quilts . . . quilts we shall never see.

And the children, dear Lord, the children! They had harmed no one, they had no political viewpoints to inflame Timothy McVeigh, they were innocent. How could anyone be so cruel, so evil? The pictures are still in my mind, the loss still painful.

Months later, when I was asked to make a memorial quilt for the "Sewing Comfort Out of Grief" traveling exhibit to honor the

children who perished that day, I couldn't get started soon enough. Sitting down with pencil and paper, I began the process of creating my memorial offering. I chose to look at the children in happier times, so my drawings of them show them at the beach, skating, decorating their Christmas trees, etc. Around them are appliquéd flowers, toys, ribbons, "kid" stuff in wonderful colors. The drawings and poem are in black ink on an off-white background. Why? Because the children are gone, leaving us only with memories. They left a hole in our lives that never can be filled by anyone or anything else.

As I stitched, I suddenly realized that what had happened to us in my hometown and within our country, and how we felt about it, is exactly what happened to families in Ireland, Afghanistan, Israel, and *so* many other places around the world. Why, I kept asking the quiet room in which I sewed. Why do we do this? Why do we place little value on the most precious things in our lives? I'm not wise enough or smart enough to find the answer. All I can do is talk through my quilts and hope they bring some hope, some laughter, some healing where it is badly needed. Perhaps that healing will enable someone else to find answers to those questions and ways to solve those problems. I certainly hope so.

*"Let the little children come to Me,*
*and do not forbid them;*
*for of such is the kingdom of heaven."*
*Matthew 19:14*

# Men and Women of Biblical Proportions

*as told by Ruth Harris to Judy Howard*

"Mom," Chantelle Cory sobbed over the phone to Ruth Harris that hot August afternoon in 2002. "The doctor just diagnosed me with Multiple Sclerosis."

What could be more devastating than a life sentence of debilitating and crippling MS in which nerve and muscle function is eventually lost. As mother and daughter processed the news over the next several weeks, they desperately sought an uplifting project to help them focus positively on whatever the future would bring.

Having just won two first places at the OKC Winter Quilt Show, veteran quilter Ruth brainstormed with her daughter, "Maybe we could contact our quilting friends nationwide to make quilts representing each woman in the Bible. We could put it together for an exhibit. That would give us something worthwhile to occupy our minds."

"Studying the Bible characters to find out how God changed them always fascinated me," Chantelle readily agreed. "We might even gain insight into our own predicament." They agreed that a little divine intervention would be welcome.

For the next two years, Chantelle and Ruth worked feverishly to complete their Women of Biblical Proportion touring quilt exhibit. They published a CD and donated a portion of their profits to MS research. People so enjoyed Women of Biblical Proportion that Ruth and Chantelle developed a second project, Men of Biblical Proportion, which debuted at the 2005 Houston International Quilt Show.

God began to work in Ruth's life as she curated these exhibits. Visiting with me after a Central Oklahoma Quilt Guild meeting, Ruth joyfully shared, "On July 20, 2005, I was miraculously saved. My experience also led to the salvation of my husband who'd been an atheist. I never could have dreamed it would be such a wonderful life-changing event." Ruth and her husband were both baptized in September, 2005. Family and friends shared in this monumental occasion. "I can't wait to see what God has planned for our lives and for the exhibits!" Ruth told me.

Ruth graciously lent me her two OKC Murrah memorial quilts to exhibit at my book signings. Her Heartbreak in the Heartland showed Oklahoma City's heart bursting in two immediately after the April 19, 1995, bombing. From the heart came baby shoes, toys, rescue workers, the Ryder truck, a clock stuck at 9:02 and a US flag.

The street names were penned around the perimeter of the fabric city grid. The airport in the corner of the quilt shows the volunteers pouring in. Even the president was depicted planting a tree at the White House. Actual police crime tape bordered the debris. The bolt from the Ryder truck was divinely included at the bottom of the quilt ten years before the headlines proclaimed its discovery.

The colors of the ribbons worn by workers and families during their grieving made up the border blocks—blue for courage, yellow for the missing, white for innocence lost, purple for the children and teal for healing. A huge needle and streaming teal ribbon at the bottom of the heart showed God's beginning the healing process of stitching the brokenness into beauty. The quilt front was covered in black tulle to symbolize the cloud hanging over the city—the veil of death. For the backing, Ruth pieced together a chaotic cityscape pictorial fabric and another calico symbolizing people fleeing. Three bomb bursts document the devastating details.

Ruth's second memorial quilt, Their Spirits Remain, shows the rubble of the Murrah Building two years after the blast. There she sewed a chain link memorial fence as well as 168 tiny four-patch heads with bodies to depict those who departed. Twelve guardian angels fly in the fabric sky. At the top, Ruth quilted God's hands reaching down to heal and comfort.

Ruth finds it quite ironic that in doing something she saw as being more to help her daughter's illness, God graphically displayed His divine providence and grace for Ruth's own life in her quilts ten years before He revealed Himself personally to her as Savior, Comforter and Healer of her soul.

*"You have turned for me my mourning into dancing . . . to the end that my glory may sing praise to You and not be silent. O LORD my God, I will give thanks to You forever."*
*Psalm 30:11-12*

# *Flaming Hot Cowboy Star*

### *by Lisa Foley*

Lisa Foley was inspired to create this quilt twenty years after she stumbled across this information in the OSU Library:

"OSU's mascot Pistol Pete is modeled after Frank Eaton (1860-1958) who left Connecticut at the age of eight with his family who settled on a homestead in Kansas. Legend tells that Eaton, one of the fastest gunmen of his day, put five of the eleven notches on his .45 Colt tracking down a group of Confederates who murdered his father when Frank was eight. The other six notches were accumulated when Pistol Pete was riding as a U.S. Deputy marshal for Judge Issac C. Parker, the 'hanging Judge' of the U.S. district court of the western district of Arkansas."

After retiring as a federal lawman, Eaton participated in the Oklahoma Land Run of 1889 and homesteaded in Perkins. Eaton replaced the A&M tiger as official school mascot after leading the 1923 Armistice Parade in Stillwater. OAMC students were tired of the tiger mascot (after the Princeton mascot, the alma mater of OAMC president R.J. Barker), and felt Eaton, with steel gray, waist length braids and drooping moustache, symbolized the 'Aggies' perfectly."

# *The Oklahoma Quilt*

### *by Karen Judd*

"I just had a Technicolor dream of the quilt I'm going to create for the Oklahoma Centennial," Karen Judd told her husband over morning coffee. "It'll include the state seal and map surrounded by cowboy boots, guitar, football, space shuttle, Indian headdress, survivor tree, Rt. 66, oil derricks and buffalo. Then I thought I'd include autographs of celebrity Oklahomans. Any ideas on names?

"Sounds fascinating," her husband said. "How about Carl Albert, Bob Wills, Douglas Edwards, Warren Spahn, Ralph Blane, Darla Hood, Stuart Roosa, Robert S. Kerr, Will Rogers, Wiley Post, Ben Johnson, Bill Bright, Willard Stone, Lon Chaney Jr., K.S.Boots Adams, Jim Thorpe, Gene Autry, Norma Smallwood, Frank Phillips, Tom Mix, Van Helfin, Leon McAulitte, Pepper Martin, Don Porter, Angie Debo. . . and don't forget my favorite Okies Lous L'Amour, Dizzy Dean, Roger Miller, Mickey Mantle and Woody Guthry."

Two years later Karen's dream became a prize-winning reality at the 2006 OKC Winter Quilt Show and will tour Oklahoma during the Centennial in 2007.

# 1924 Family Album Quilt

*by Judy Howard*

"This is Grandmother's Family Album quilt," Karen said as she spread out the 1924 embroidery embellished quilt with names of her ancestors. "It was made to welcome my dad into the clan before his birth.

"And here's my great-great-grandparent's wedding quilt dated 1877," Karen said as I examined the vibrant red and green pieced Tulips.

"Do you have any stories about your family for my next *Heavenly Patchwork* book I'm writing about Oklahoma's history as told through women and their quilts?" I asked as I sorted through the dozen quilts Karen brought for me to purchase.

"I have a dome-top trunk full of memorabilia like my great-grandparent's wedding picture and marriage certificate dated December 21, 1898, Ardmore, Indian Territory along with christening bonnets, baby rings, four Indian Territory homestead certificates, oil and gas leases, school pictures, farm leases, 1912 mortgage, 1904 Abstract of Title, Aetna farm insurance policy for lightning, funeral and commencement programs," Karen said as she dumped the contents of a manila envelope on the table. She told me about the rocking chair made for her granddad in 1924 and the round oak table and patterned back chairs she had inherited.

"My favorite item is this hysterical newspaper clipping showing my great aunt dressed in her long white dress with ax in hand in a woodchoppers contest dated August 11, 1908 on the Washita River," Karen said with a giggle.

I thanked Karen for showing me her priceless treasures and for posing in front of the Tulip wedding quilt for a picture to capture her family's heritage documented in her quilts.

---

*"Beloved, I pray that you may prosper in all things and be in health, just as your soul prospers."*
*3John 1:2*

# This is Your Life

### by Gayla White

I'd never seen my grandparents speechless before, nor had I ever seen Granddad cry. But tears of happiness filled their eyes as they examined each unique square of the quilt made by their daughters and granddaughters to celebrate their fiftieth wedding anniversary. There were soon tears in everyone's eyes as my grandparents sat silently gazing at the names of their family and pictures of their lives colorfully embroidered on white blocks and lovingly stitched together between calico strips.

Wish I knew what memories ran through my grandparent's minds as they inspected the symbols of their lives - the flag representing our American heritage and Grandad's service in World War II, golden wheat, the bold "T" of Granddad's cattle brand, double gold wedding rings, and a child in a wash tub. . . "Where have the years gone?" was surely one of their thoughts.

Grandchildren searched for and traced their names on the quilt proudly displayed on a wall in my grandparent's den. Grown children reminisced about long forgotten stories brought freshly to mind by the embroidered pictures. Visitors were invited to share the memories captured in the fabric.

The quilt has passed down to me. It adds a cozy charm to the room, and my heart, as it lays folded across the windowsill of my home office. When I look at the quilt my mind is filled with affectionate memories of holidays and summers spent on the farm helping Grandma pick fresh green beans for dinner, swimming in the watering hole, laying at the top of the stairs with my cousins on Christmas Eve to peek through the banister in at attempt to catch Santa, Saturday trips to town that always ended at Dairy Queen, and swaying back and forth on the rope swing by the road. Just like snuggling up in a quilt on a cold winter night, my childhood recollections wrap around my heart with warmth and security.

*You will be secure, because there is hope;*
*you will look about you and take your rest in safety. Job 11:18*

# Thimble Thumping Mama

### as told by Earlene Roach
### to Judy Howard

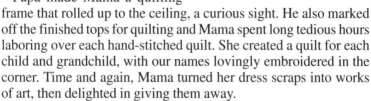

Mama was never without her thimble, for she was always piecing or quilting. I got thumped on my head with that thimble when I was unruly.

Papa made Mama a quilting frame that rolled up to the ceiling, a curious sight. He also marked off the finished tops for quilting and Mama spent long tedious hours laboring over each hand-stitched quilt. She created a quilt for each child and grandchild, with our names lovingly embroidered in the corner. Time and again, Mama turned her dress scraps into works of art, then delighted in giving them away.

Mama was a Sunday school teacher and looked forward to the weekly quilting bees at her Methodist church in Ft. Smith, Arkansas. I'll never forget the Bible stories she taught me as she pieced my dress scraps together. Sleeping under those warm coverlets in the winter was pure heaven. I felt safe, secure and loved as I said my nightly prayers and Mama tucked the quilt up around my ears.

When she was eighty-one years old and her eyesight was failing, Mama finished her last quilt. The entire family joined in to help her complete a white and blue centennial quilt. Mama's daughters embroidered the blocks, Mama's sister stitched them together, and, as always, Papa marked the quilting lines. With a favorite thimble on her finger, Mama hand-quilted her final treasure.

Mama gave us much more than beautiful quilts through the years. By her example, she gave a legacy of cooperation, thrift, craftsmanship, generosity, and love. What a beautiful Godly heritage to pass on to one's family.

*"Two are better than one,*
*because they have a good reward for their labor.*
*For if they fall, one will lift up his companion."*
*Ecclesiastes 4:9-10 NKJ*

# Oh Ye of Little Faith

## by Judy Howard

One Saturday morning in June of 1996 at Buchanan's Antique Flea Market, I spotted a stunning hand-painted Indian quilt by a renowned Seminole Creek artist. Even though it was contemporary, I was tempted to buy it for resale in my antique store. But I was running late to open the shop and my bank account was almost in the red, so I rushed on to work.

Between customers, I researched the artist via the phone and realized the potential. I prayed for wisdom and promised God that if I did get it, I'd give the quilt back to Him to multiply like the little boy's fishes and loaves to feed His children. Then I panicked thinking; *It's been two hours. Someone else will have snapped up such a find.*

But I couldn't even get out of the shop. Two charming ladies were taking their sweet time browsing through hundreds of quilts as I became more and more agitated and impatient with each wasted moment. Finally, I couldn't contain myself another second. "I know this sounds a bit unorthodox," I told the ladies, "but I have a slight emergency. Would you mind if I locked you in the shop for just a few minutes. I'll be back in fifteen minutes at the most."

"We're having a ball and wouldn't mind spending the rest of the day just looking and touching these wonderful quilts. We'd be delighted to shopsit for you," they answered.

So I locked the shop door, jumped in my van and sped the six blocks back to the fairgrounds. *Oh ye of little faith.* Of course God's quilt was there waiting for me, and He had even prearranged a lower price.

After nearly a month of further research, I was even more excited about my purchase. I mailed pictures out to my customers, as I often do, and received a call immediately with an order to purchase the quilt for eight times my cost. "Praise the Lord for another miracle." I was bragging on Him to everyone I knew and rejoicing that He had seen fit to use me in such a marvelous way to help feed His children. I had even promised Grace Rescue Mission that their check for 100% of the proceeds was in the mail.

My faith was further tested when the payment didn't arrive the next day as promised, but only after two weeks of my fretting and worrying. When the payment finally arrived, I chastised myself again, *Oh ye of little faith.*

> *"Ask, and it will be given to you; seek, and you will find; knock, and it will be opened to you." Matthew 7:7*

# Promise Me, Finish My Quilts

*by Sharon Anne Lindahl*

"My arm is really hurting," my mother Nandell Stiles said. I stood to be able to read the heart monitor beside my mother's bed.

Being a nurse, I advised her, "Take a nitro, Mom. Your heart skipped a few beats. That's causing the pain." Mom complied. I pushed the call bell to notify Mother's nurse.

"It's still hurting," my mother complained.

I stared hard at the heart monitor, wanting it to have gotten word that the medicine was now in place, wanting it to give us better news.

"Take another nitro," I told my mother as I called the nurse again to keep her up to speed on my mother's condition.

This second pill didn't work, either. "Now it hurts in my shoulder," Mom complained. My mother had begun to sweat, a sign of severe pain.

On the monitor, I saw a sign that things were getting even worse. *Oh no*, I thought. Fear drying my mouth, I called the nurse a third time, frantic now. "You'd better get up here with IV morphine right now. Oh, God save her," I screamed, watching the line of continuous PVC'S. I heard running down the hall to bring my mother lifesaving relief from the crushing pain.

"Mom, hang on. Hang on. It's the pain that kills you. She's coming. The nurse is bringing you strong pain medicine right now." Evidently, Mom was having her second heart attack in eight days.

My mother grabbed for me with her right hand. With sweat beading her face and agony evident in her eyes, she whispered, "Promise me. Promise me."

Unable to speak, I nodded over and over. Yes to anything. Everything.

"Promise me. Finish my quilts," she said.

I pictured my mother's neatly folded stack of handmade quilt tops, patiently waiting for her magic quilting. Then my mother's pain was too great. She no longer could speak. A nurse pushed me aside as she rushed in to administer lifesaving medications. Other nurses came. Dr. Jones arrived. They asked me to leave the room.

I went to the little chapel by the lobby and knelt in prayer, asking God to preserve Mom's life. Olive Flynn, mother's long time friend and volunteer at the hospital that day, knelt beside me to pray. Olive put her hand on my shoulder. "I've already called your sister. Beth said she'd be right over. You need to call your dad and the rest of your family."

I told Olive what my mother made me promise. She shook her head, tears glistening, "Only Nan would lie in agony on her deathbed and make sure her wonderful quilts would be finished."

Only it wasn't Mom's deathbed. As more and more of our family arrived, Mom began to respond. The heart arrhythmias slowed and stopped. The pain medicine and other life-giving medicines began their work. The nurses called the family in, two at a time, to see Mom.

Too exhausted to speak, my mother merely opened her eyes, nodded her head, and with a little smile, dropped off to sleep.

Was it that prayer in the chapel that saved her? I believe so. The prayer of the faithful moves the hand of God. For God promises us in Matthew 21:22 "If you believe, you will receive what you ask for in prayer." In Mark 11:24, God promises us, "Therefore I tell you, whatever you ask for in prayer, believe you have received it, and it will be yours."

What was my prayer that day in that little chapel? "Lord, let my mother live and thrive so she will be able to finish those last six quilts for her grandchildren." She did. I helped.

## United Outpouring of Love
*by Marg Layton*

Yesterday I delivered a cooperative quilt made of seventy-two pink Log Cabin blocks for Laurie Shepstone who is courageously fighting for her life against breast cancer.

Members of the Machine Quilters Professional list individually contributed and signed the blocks to let Lauri know they were praying for God's richest blessings for her. I had the privilege of binding the quilt after Kim Brunner machine-quilted it.

Although Laurie and I never had met, I wanted to be the one to wrap her in the arms of love. After driving for an hour to reach her home, I was humbled as I experienced her beautiful courageous spirit. She was overwhelmed at the outpouring of love from machine quilters from Canada, the United States, and Great Britain.

*"Therefore comfort each other and edify one another . . ."*
*1 Thessolonians 5:11*

# The Wildnerness Shall Blossom as the Rose of Sharon

*by Judy Howard*

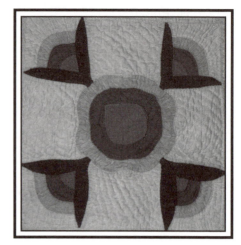

In writing dozens of stories about Oklahoma homesteaders, I'm most impressed by the indomitable Sooner spirit of the brave women who forsook their homelands, suffering unbelievable hardships to claim 160 acres of the Indian Territory barren wilderness opened up for settling in 1889. Can you imagine the anxiety when you learned that 50,000 other homeseekers lined up along the borders of the Unassigned Lands waiting for the resounding gunshot to begin the race to claim only 10,000 tracts available? Again in 1891 the scene was repeated with three to one odds as the Sac and Fox Country became available.

Can you feel the tension mounting as thousands of families from Russia, Europe and America gathered to wait on the boundary guarded by United States cavalry for the signal? All shared a common dream of making a fresh start on this raw frontier. One day after the Land Rush, central Oklahoma was settled and towns sprung to life as the three cultures—Indian, cowboy and homesteader—intermingled.

One such Oklahoman was Dr. J. Anges Gillis who settled in Frederick, Oklahoma to open his medical office. In 1999 I purchased this Rose of Sharon quilt from his daughter Lois Hall's estate of fifty years near downtown Oklahoma City. Lois was born in that new frontier in 1894. I wish I had questioned her then about the blood, sweat and tears required to change that barren wasteland into the lush green of cultivated acres.

The spiritual analogy is clear of Christ's nurturing and constant flow of life-giving water essential to transform the unfruitful desert of the sinful heart to blossom as a rose. I donated this Rose of Sharon quilt to Oklahoma Baptist University. It appraised and is available for $3000 payable to OBU. (405-878-2718)

*"The wilderness and the wasteland shall be glad for them, and the desert shall rejoice and blossom as the rose; it shall blossom abundantly and rejoice, even with joy and singing. The glory of Lebanon shall be given to it, the excellence of Carmel and Sharon. They shall see the glory of the Lord, the excellency of our God."*
Isaiah 35:1-2

## Calico Dress Lives Again as Mariner's Compass
### by Judy Howard

In 1999, Abigail Ford returned from settling her grandmother's estate in Milford, Connecticut and brought this breath-taking Mariner's Compass into Buckboard Quilts to sell.

"Can you believe this quilt is made from an old dress? My great-great-great-grandmother on my father's side made this quilt in 1850 in Yonkers New York," Abigail explained when I asked her the history.

Ardelia Foote Gilmore bought the calico in 1834 and made it into a dress before she died May 12th, 1834. Her daughter Mary Gilmore Smith cut the dress up to piece and quilt this Mariner's Compass before she was married in January of 1853. The backing was hand woven by Mary's grandmother Ruth Smith.

"This quilt was passed down to the Hutchersons, Schropshires, Fords and now to me," Abigail said as she pointed out the initials on the back corner and handed me the note written by her grandmother documenting the provenance.

Like the boy who gave his loaves and fishes to God to multiply to feed the 5000, I gave this quilt back to God by donating it to my alma mater Oklahoma Baptist University. It appraised and is available for $17,500 paid directly to OBU. (405-878-2718)

*"And He took the five loaves and the two fish, and looking up to heaven, He blessed and broke and gave the loaves to the disciples; and the disciples gave to the multitudes. So they all ate and were filled." Matthew 14:19b-20a*

# Barn Raising

### by Kim Brunner

"And what did you bring to work on, Kim?" Michelle asked as we settled into our quilter's retreat cottage last winter on a weekend getaway.

"I brought these Aunt Gracie fabrics and scrappy white prints to make a king-sized Barn Raising Log Cabin," I said, pulling out scissors and fabric. "I don't know why I chose the pattern or where I can even use it. With two large golden retrievers who slobber, I'd never put it on our bed and we don't have a wall big enough to hang it. But this voice in my head keeps bellowing, 'Barn Raising Log Cabin! Hurry!'"

By mid-summer, the quilt was almost completed and I still hadn't a clue why I was making it. Then one Sunday our pastor talked about the gifts of the Holy Spirit we're given and that it's our responsibility to use those gifts in the church. At the end of the sermon, Pastor Jim announced that the owner of a large construction company offered to donate half the labor, money and materials required to finish the education wing if others would do the rest. Jim pointed out that money and volunteers were needed to help hang sheet rock, paint and cook for the workers. "What we need is an old-fashioned barn raising."

I almost fell out of the pew. *You need an old fashioned barn raising? Hey, I've got one of those at home, and you can have it!* At that moment, I wouldn't have been surprised to see God Himself sitting in the pew behind me chuckling about how well His plans were working. He'd put a bee in my bonnet last winter because He knew our church would need a quilt to raise money. I tried my best not to disrupt the service by laughing hysterically at God's great sense of humor. Joyfully I drove home, realizing for the first time that quilting was a gift I could offer to benefit the church.

I finished the sixty hours of quilting and loathsome binding on the quilt the night before the sale. Crosshatching the border corners provided the perfect place to hide the words "Farmington Lutheran Church 2005." My quilt sold for $2000 which should pay for lots of crayons and supplies needed to furnish classrooms.

Next time the inner voice starts bellowing, I'll not hesitate or question—just instantly obey—knowing God has a plan to use my gifts for His Kingdom's work.

*"As each one has received a gift, minister it to one another, as good stewards of the manifold grace of God." I Peter 4:10*

### Dustin Hoffman Made My Day

*by Judy Howard*

"Where have you been?" my husband Bill asked. "And why are you getting home from the shop so late? I was beginning to worry about you."

I barely knew where to start. How would Bill believe that just as I was turning out the lights and about to lock the front door of my quilt shop after a slow day, four women in shorts scrambled through the door. I welcomed them, and then in walked a short man in a black OSU tee shirt and blue jeans, holding hands with a small girl. My jaw must have dropped a mile and I was nearly speechless when I recognized Dustin Hoffman.

I explained to Bill, who doesn't keep up on the movies, that today had been Dustin Hoffman's last day in town with Tom Cruise filming *Rainman.*

I tried to steady my knocking knees and said a quick prayer for help before I could properly welcome this famous man. Dustin was most gracious and understanding since he probably gets that reaction everywhere he goes. Over the next two hours, I began to relax, and in the end, we had a ball, pulling quilts off the walls and spreading them out on beds for inspection. It looked like a whirlwind had gone through my usually tidy shop before they left.

"What was he like?" Bill asked, actually putting down his paper.

I explained that Dustin was totally down-to-earth, warm and friendly, with a great sense of humor. And what charm! He was amazingly considerate, patient and kind to me and the women with him. He invited their opinions and then, slyly, surprised each of them with a quilt as a gift. In the end, he'd picked out seventeen of my best quilts. I bagged them up for him to take with him, except for one which I promised to ship as soon as I could remove a stain.

"Why in the world would he want seventeen quilts?" Bill wondered. The same thought had crossed my mind even though I'd seen his name listed in our *Maine Antique Digest* as attending the premier antique auctions back East. My guess was that he was planning to keep his favorites and give the rest away as gifts.

Immediately, Bill wanted to know which quilts Dustin Hoffman selected.

*167---Faith*

It was fun remembering Dustin's joy as he bought a great Sunbonnet Sue and Overall Bill quilt for his daughter. He'd also bought a fabulous signed and dated 1931 Amish Irish Chain crib quilt in solid blue, pink and white that Bill and I'd found last year in Lancaster, Pennsylvania. I'd almost cried having to part with that prize since I was positive I'd never find another one to equal it.

He also chose a YoYo spread, two 1800's handwoven overshot coverlets, a Trip around the World, Dresden Plate, three Wedding Rings, Tulip Go Round, Star, Hawaiian Wedding Appliqué, blue Ocean Waves and three Flower Garden Quilts. "He had exquisite taste."

"Obviously so! It sounds like Dustin made your day."

Bill was certainly right about that.

The whole time Dustin and his entourage were in the shop, I was asking God to put a desire in Dustin's heart to buy lots of quilts. And God answered beyond my wildest expectations. *Blessings never cease when you ask believing*, I thought as I headed for the kitchen to fix dinner for my starving man. God taught me the power of prayer that day.

> *"And whatever things you ask in prayer,*
> *believing, you will receive."*
> Matthew 21:22

## God's Valentine's Day Surprise
### by Judy Howard

"But I don't want to go to the lake and leave you alone on Valentine's Day," my husband pleaded, obviously feeling guilty.

"Oh please, go on without me. I'll be fine. I can't afford to close the shop right after mailing out my advertisements. Really, it's okay. Have a great time." I'll admit I felt forsaken, since it is a day we associate with spending with our love-mates.

I'm so glad I didn't escape to the lake that Valentine's Day in 2002. I would have missed God's infinitely greater blessing. On the way to work, I followed God's prompting, and stopped by the nursing home to visit my ninety and ninety-six-year-old friends Ethel and James.

I was having a wonderful conversation with Ethel and her daughter Janet while James snoozed in the next bed. James' health was declining rapidly, and the family was praying he wouldn't suffer much longer.

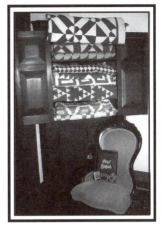

Fifteen minutes later, Janet bolted out of her chair and ran to her father's bed. "Oh my gosh! He's quit breathing!" she said, startling us with her announcement. "He's gone, Mother . . . peacefully and quietly in his sleep just as we prayed."

We called the head nurse and several relatives, and soon the room was abuzz with activity. I prayed with Janet and Ethel for God's peace and comfort to calm their shattered nerves, and we prayed for strength to deal with the decisions to be made.

I held Ethel's hand until the rest of the family arrived and helped the best I could. Then I rushed to my shop to open two hours late, sure the day was a waste for my lagging February sales. Within a few moments of my flipping on lights, a customer from California entered. Fifteen minutes later, he purchased the three quilts from the Clara Rosenthal Weitzenhoffer Estate (story on page 10 of *Heavenly Patchwork I*) I had given to God to multiply to feed His children. As I was writing my check for the $4200 quilt sale to Grace Rescue Mission, this California customer surprised me by buying another valuable quilt to boost my sagging sales.

I fell to my knees with joy, thanking God for the best Valentine's Day gift I've ever received, and for welcoming James home. God had placed me where He could use me in the family's time of need and rewarded me doubly for my obedience. I'm so grateful I followed the Holy Spirit's prompting and was able to help.

God is always working behind the scenes, orchestrating great and mighty deeds that the world may know His love. I shudder to think of the blessings I would have missed in that four hours had I not been listening and obedient. There is no greater joy and privilege than to be used by God.

> *"But without faith it is impossible to please Him,*
> *for he who comes to God must believe that He is,*
> *that He is a rewarder of those who diligently seek Him."*
> *Hebrews 11:6*

*169---Faith*

# *Jessica Lange Loves Quilts Too*

*by Judy Howard*

Steve LePort and his wife came into Buckboard Antique Quilts before Christmas in 1989. "Congratulations on winning the Academy Award for cosmetology for *Beetlejuice*," I told Steve. "That's awesome for our hometown boy to earn such a prestigious and coveted award. We're so proud of you," I gushed. Then realizing they came in to shop, I asked, "How may I help you?"

"We'd like to find quilts for my mom for Christmas," Steve explained. "She's always loved them, but never found time to make them. I love them, too, and figure they'll become mine when she's ready to part with them."

As we spread out a few on the bed, Steve chose his favorites. "I just returned from working with Jessica Lange on a set in Chicago," he told me. "She has a fabulous collection and was buying quilts like crazy. Bet she'd love your shop. I could mail her your business card if you like."

"Would I ever!" I said, running to get my card. "We do a huge mail order business and I send out picture packets daily. I'd be delighted to add her name to my mailing list." I thanked him profusely for offering and whispered a quick prayer that Jessica Lange would become my customer, but promptly pushed it out of my mind as a remote possibility.

Was I ever shocked when Jessica personally called the following February. She ordered several museum quality floral appliquéd quilts. Over the next ten years, God blessed me beyond my wildest dreams through Jessica's quilt orders. He's always so faithful to give His children the desires of their hearts when it's for their good.

> *"Delight yourself also in the LORD,*
> *and He shall give you the desires of your heart."*
> *Psalm 37:4*

## The Julia Roberts?

*by Judy Howard*

One spring afternoon in 1997, I received an unbelievable phone call at Buckboard Antique Quilts. "This is Julia Roberts. I'd like to order some quilts," the voice crooned.

Sure, I thought. Someone's playing games with me. No way would America's number one sweetheart be contacting me—much less in person. It must be a prank.

"And which quilts were you interested in?" I asked in my coolest most unaffected voice, waiting for the punchline.

"I'd like a couple of Double Wedding Ring quilts for wedding shower gifts . . . Numbers 4053 and 3994. How soon can you ship them out?" the person continued.

"They are in stock, and may I add that you have exquisite taste in quilts? Is Priority Mail this afternoon quick enough?" I asked. "Where would you like them shipped?"

When she told me the Hollywood shipping address, I was speechless. *Praise the Lord! It really is Julie Roberts calling.*

Over the next five years, Julia proved to be a loyal customer, and I always got a little thrill each time she called to place another order.

*" . . . that at the name of Jesus every knee should bow . . . "*
*Philippians 2:10a*

## Hugs

*by Steve Belcher*

My young daughter Ali eloquently enlightened us that our resident feline was "trying to give us hugs" when she rubbed against our legs. With this in mind, I thought about an inanimate object that symbolizes love — the quilt.

I'm the proud possessor of Grandmother Hettie's elaborate Flower Pot quilt, hand-pieced from thousands of diamonds. A surprise cool snap sent me in search of her quilt, beckoning me like an old friend. Snuggling under its familiar comfort, I remembered my daughter's comment about hugs. Hettie's labor of love wasn't only to provide future generations with a beautiful keepsake, but to be sure each recipient continued receiving "warm hugs" long after she was gone.

*He has sent me to heal the brokenhearted . . .*
*to comfort all who mourn. Isaiah 61:1-2*

# My Birthday Gift for Jesus

### by Marg Layton

Our church scheduled a special night to tie quilts for WIN House (Women In Need shelter for abused women). Our Relief Society decided to collect and donate gently used clothing, household items, games, books, and toys for the temporary guests of WIN House during the Christmas season, along with making them quilts. These gifts would help them begin a new life away from the abuse and fear they had known.

Everyone knows I'm a quiltaholic. Mention the word quilt to me, and I'm immediately geared for action. I agreed to come help tie quilts, armed with my trusty rulers, curved needles, darning needles, wool, finger cots and scissors.

I remembered a Christmas fifty years ago my dear mother taught me the true meaning of giving. In 1955 during the Hungarian Revolution on Christmas morning, we opened our gifts and were waiting for the turkey to be roasted for Christmas dinner. This year would be different with only our immediate family present since the cousins couldn't come.

Mom was listening to Christmas carols on the radio and heard an announcement that refugees from Hungary had arrived with no place to go for Christmas. The radio announcer pleaded for someone to invite a family with four girls to share their Christmas dinner. Mom instructed Dad to warm up the car and fetch our special dinner guests.

Then Mom called her four daughters together. "We're about to experience the best Christmas ever," she said. "I've invited for dinner a family with four girls who fled their country in Europe with nothing but the clothes on their backs hoping for a better life here. Since there's no time to run out to buy gifts, I want each of you to pick out your favorite toy and wrap it to give the girls so they, too, can have a Merry Christmas." Mom explained that if we gave our very best from our hearts, we would experience a wonderful Christmas we'd never forget.

We obediently went to our bedrooms and chose our very best. I searched through my doll collection. My favorite ones were the twin rubber dolls, complete with the clothing Mom had patiently sewn for them. I couldn't keep one of them for myself or that wouldn't be giving from the heart. I wrapped them both along with the suitcase that contained their clothes. Lovingly, I handed the package to Renatta who was my age. Since we did not know their language, we just said, "For you, with love." I'm sure they understood. We played together after sharing our dinner with them and experienced an unforgettable Christmas.

As I thought about those refugees, I decided to give my very best to someone at WIN House this year by making a special quilt and sharing my testimony of that Christmas in 1955. Because the quilt needed to be finished by tomorrow night, I rushed downstairs to look through my stash of material. I grabbed red and green fabrics and a pretty Christmas poinsettia print and hurried upstairs to cut the fabric into the size I needed. Three hours later, the top was completed. I quickly cut batting, soaked it in the washer and threw it in the dryer. Then I loaded the quilt on my longarm machine and quilted until midnight. My husband never complained about his tardy dinner when I told him what I was doing.

The next morning I arose early to make the label and sew the binding. I completed the quilt before noon. Talk about a miracle! I usually don't complete a quilt in a day and a half, but this is one I was proud to give. I knew it was divinely inspired because I barely had enough red and green fabric on hand. My life had been blessed and I was grateful to share with others.

> *"... inasmuch as you did it to one of the least of these*
> *My brethren, you did it to Me.'"*
> *Matthew 25:40*


## The Woman Who Made the Quilts

*by Carolyn Rowe*

The headline in the Houston Chronicle inviting quilters to come to the International Quilt Festival brought back memories of that wonderful day long ago when Mother and I attended.

Mother began quilting in 1972 and made 120 quilts until her arthritic fingers prevented it. She created quilts for three generations, including granddogs.

The memories that simple headline evoke are more precious now that Mother doesn't remember quilting. I framed a sample of her work with her thimble. She often admires it and the "woman who made it." Though I'm crushed she doesn't identify with that woman, she'll always live on through her quilts and the legacy of love she gave us.

> *"This is My commandment,*
> *that you love one another as I have loved you.*
> *John 15:12*

*173---Faith*

# Stitching and Singing

*by Judy Howard*

On a steamy August morning at a moving sale in Nichols Hills, I met a precious ninety-year-old lady. When I asked the homeowner if she had any quilts or quilt stories, she explained that she cherished her quilts and never would sell them. However, she suggested that her mom Edna, who was helping out at the sales desk, might have some quilt stories to share.

Indeed she did! Edna well remembered her mother Ada Wasson Weatherall, born in 1888 in Arkansas, singing her lungs out as she quilted. "Mom always sang her favorite hymns, praising God for His blessings, and she sang especially loud when she was happy. She was happiest when quilting. As we played nearby, we joined her in singing and reciting her favorite Bible verses.

"Whichever quilt was in process was mounted on a frame hanging from the ceiling in our living-dining-kitchen room on our farm outside Cordell, Oklahoma. At mealtime, the quilt was hoisted heavenward to free up valuable space for cooking and eating in our crowded farmhouse. Mama insisted on using #7 needles so she could take the tiniest of stitches and win the blue ribbons at the county fair," Edna shared.

"I'll never forget jumping on those feather mattresses and submerging myself beneath those warm quilts in the wintertime when the forty-mile-an-hour northerlies whistled through our log cabin. It was such a cozy comfort. I loved to trace the outline of the patterns and look for familiar calicos from my old dresses. The Ten Commandment and State Bird and Flower quilts became learning tools as Mom tutored us when we were sick at home."

Edna concluded, "Mama instilled in each of her nine children her love of God and His Word. She also instilled in us an appreciation of the fine quilts she left every one of us as a legacy of her love."

*"You shall teach them diligently to your children,
and shall talk of them when you sit in your house,
when you walk by the way,
when you lie down, and when you rise up."
Deuteronomy 6:7*

*Family Roots*
as told by
*Mildred Chenoweth*
*to Judy Howard*

Word had gotten out that the next star was being born in a third-grade musical production of *Sound of Music*. This petite little blonde had just sung in her grade school music teacher's wedding, and everyone was mesmerized by her amazing voice, poise and beauty. Roy and Mildred Chenoweth traveled from Hinton, Oklahoma to Broken Arrow to see their eight-year-old granddaughter Kristie play what they thought was a bit part in a school play.

"My gosh, honey, she's got the lead. Can you believe our little Kristie is the star?" Mildred whispered to her husband. "I had no idea she could sing and dance that well. All those ballet and music lessons really paid off."

"She's growing up so fast," Roy added, a mixture of pride and sorrow across his face. "Can this be the same little girl who stayed with us last summer?" Already he was planning how they could take Kristie out for an ice cream cone afterwards to celebrate her performance.

Unfortunately, backstage was a mob scene with a dozen agents scrambling to sign Kristen Chenoweth to manage her brilliant future. But Kristie's heart has remained humble, sweet and loyal to her family and grandparents. She insists on visiting twice a year between shows on Broadway or in Hollywood.

Kristen has won a Tony award for her performance in *You're a Good Man Charlie Brown* with her lead song of *My Philosophy*. And she's performed to a sellout audience in Carnegie Hall before heading to Hollywood to film *Bewitched* and *West Wing*. Kristen is a graduate of Oklahoma City University where, at her graduation, still only 4'11" she danced, sang opera, played the piano, and acted her way into everyone's heart. Her relatives were there to cheer her on.

Kristen also sang for her grandpa Roy's ninetieth birthday retirement party held at the Cherokee Trading Post on Route 66. She really brought down the house when she said, "You know you're a redneck when you hold your family reunions at a truck stop."

She's received awards so often you might think she'd be immune. Not so. She still cried for joy when her grandma Mildred gave her a pink handmade Grandmother's Fan as her legacy quilt for Christmas. She was really touched and said how special and loved she feels that her grandma would create something so beautiful just for her.

Mildred enjoyed making Grandmother's Fan quilts for all three granddaughters, but admitted she never wanted to see that pattern again. Mildred's favorite quilt was the Chinese Lantern she received as a wedding gift in 1935 from Roy's mother. The Oklahoma Heritage Group came to Hinton and registered her wedding quilt and photographed it for their *Oklahoma Heritage Quilts* book. Roy's grandmother's 1860's Eagle quilt she made for her three Civil War soldier sons became the cover photo for the book.

Mildred remembers learning to quilt when she was seventeen. Cora Chenoweth brought Mildred dress scraps and taught her the basic stitches.

Roy's favorite of Mildred's quilts was the one she made six years ago with pictures of their eight children, her mom and dad's wedding picture, plus individual portraits of her parents. "But you have to look quick when Mildred is quilting. She makes them and gives them away so fast, I can't keep track," Roy said.

Mildred and Roy have lived in the same town their entire lives, and Mildred's gone to the same First Baptist church since she was born. They marveled how, in their tiny German farming community, they never met before their first blind date. No doubt Roy's dad brought his plow shears to Mildred's dad to be sharpened and paid him in chickens and eggs back before Mildred and Roy were even born. For family outings in Red Rock Canyon, Roy's mom fixed a sunrise breakfast spread on a picnic quilt for his friends who spent the day swimming and playing Rook.

Roy remembers those as the good old days, reminiscing with his cousins and thanking God for his wonderful family.

*"I bow my knees to the Father of our Lord Jesus Christ, from whom the whole family in heaven and earth is named, that He would grant you, according to the riches of His glory to be strengthened with might through His Spirit in the inner man, that Christ may dwell in your hearts through faith; that you, being rooted and grounded in love, may be able to comprehend with all the saints what is the width and length and depth and height—to know the love of Christ which passes knowledge; that you may be filled with all the fullness of God." Ephesians 3:14-19*

# Editors & Contributors

**Bob Annesley** is a Master Artist of the Five Civilized Tribes. To purchase *Mary's Sunshine* contact annesleystudio@yahoo.com.

**Esterita Austin**, internationally award-winning quilt maker, designer and teacher, was featured on *The Sally Jesse Raphael Show* and *Simply Quilts* on HGTV, episode 1134. www.esteritaaustin.com

**Blanche Barrymore**, born to pioneer parents in Roger Mills County, writes human interest stories about her past. Blanche attended Southwest Teachers College and has two children and two grandchildren.

**Opal Baum**, born in Stephens County, OK in 1917, has three children, eight grandchildren, twenty-two great grandchildren and one great-great-grandchild.

**Kay Bishop**, B.S., M. Ed., author and Teacher/Consultant for the OK Writing Project, affiliated with the National Writing Project.

**Kim Brunner** is a national and international award-winning longarm quilter and teacher, living in MN with her husband, children, dogs, and fabric.

**Alice Caine** educated at North Central College, Naperville, IL, Gonzaga Law School and KS State University worked as an accountant. Now widowed, Alice has three children and six grandchildren and volunteers at Integris Baptist Hospital.

**Linda Carlson** has authored four books: *Roots, Feathers & Blooms, 4-Block Quilts, Their History & Pattern, Memories for Today, Tomorrow & Forever* and *The Best of 4 Blocks & More.* Linda teaches, judges and designs fabric for Benartex. www.lindacarlsonquilts.com

**Bessie Elston's** story is about her mother Mable Huckins who made quilts for all her children and grandkids and lived in Thomas, OK.

**Anna Sterling Farris**, is a happy wife, mother of three and grandmother of six who has a love of homemaking that started as a toddler while watching her grandmother piece together quilt blocks.

**Larry Fisher** lives in Norman, OK with wife Carol. A member of the Oklahoma City Territory Tellers, a professional storytellers organization, he was published in *Country Magazine* in 2005.

**Rebecca Holmberg Freeman** of Broken Arrow, OK, a retired sales representative, enjoys life as a home economist, romance novel author, musical composer, and "fun" artist.

**Lena Hamrick Frost** of Norman grew up in Ponca City, graduated from OU, and University of IL. She and husband, Ed, are parents of Jeremy and Lydia. Lena started quilting fifteen years ago.

**Delaine Gately's** family ranks first and quilting second. Her grandmother introduced her to the love of quilts through her Sunbonnet Sue. Delaine collects and makes traditional and art quilts and raises money for breast cancer through her passion for quilts.

**Zolalee Gaylor** received thimbles for her fifth birthday. Hand quilting became her passion in 1980 when she became a charter member of the COQG. She has taught at Oklahoma Quiltworks for eighteen years and has won many blue ribbons.

**Martha Green** is a professional artist with over thirty years of graphic arts and teaching experience. She has a B.F.A. from the University of OK. She was an OK State Artist in Residence for thirteen years and has participated in over 150 gallery shows and art festivals. She is most recognized as a fiber artist and has developed the *Carney Roadside School of Crazy Quilting*.

**Ruth Harris**, nationally known, award winning fiber artist, has curated invitational touring quilt exhibits of *Men and Women of Biblical Proportions* and *Voices in Fabric* besides exhibiting in many solo shows. Buy $10 CDs on wobp-mobp.org.

**Mary Jewett** lives and writes in De Soto, Kansas, just down the road from where she and her grandmother created their quilts.

**Alice Doughty Kellogg's** first quilt was an appliquéd Sunbonnet Sue made with her grandmother and hand quilted by the Mennonite in Fairview, OK. She starting seriously quilting in 1993, is President of the Edmond Quilt Guild and teaches at My Sister's Quilt.

**Joy Neal Kidney**, a freelance writer, lives in West Des Moines, IA, with her husband, Guy. They have been church choir, AWANA, school, Scouting, and ESL volunteers

**Suzanne Kistler** lives in Visalia, CA, with her husband and four children and has been quilting since 1983. The Lord continually uses quilting and quilters to bless her. She cherishes the blessings of her quiltmaking friends, is a frequent contributor to quilt magazines and enjoys participating in national shows.

**Herschel Koester,** a retiree-wanna-be from Continental Airlines, restores antique clocks—preserving history with ultimate care.

**Mary Lynn Kotz**, journalist and author based in Washington D.C., has written five books, including *Rauschenberg/Art and Life* (Harry N. Abrams, Inc.), for which she won the 2005 Iowa Author Award.

**Marg Layton** owns a longarm machine quilting business, I Quilt For You, in Edmonton, Alberta. Her goal is to continue to bless others with her quilts. www.iquiltforyou.ca

**Molly Lemmons**' collection of stories about growing up in Oklahoma City in the 1950's ran for three years in OK, AR, and TX newspapers. The columns were published into a book, *Kind of Heart*, in magazines, and in *Chicken Soup for the Mother's Soul*. Her latest book, *The Passing of Paradise* was released in 2005.

**Carolyn Branch Leonard**, graduate of OKC University, President of OKC Writers and on Executive Committee of OK Writers Federation, wrote stories for best seller *In Their Name*, a state-endorsed book on the 1995 bombing in Oklahoma City. She writes for *Persimmon Hill Magazine* and as American History chair in DAR, she published a book *Patriot Ancestors*.

**Jean Lewis** worked forty-five years at a mortgage company and has made hundreds of beautiful quilts for family, friends and the Infant Crisis Center. Her biggest project was a king-size quilt for her daughter with 3666 pieces.

**Sharon Anne Lindahl**, Will Rogers Senior Center quilt leader, retired nurse and daughter to Nandell Stiles of the story *Promise Me*, lives in Richland, OK. Like her mother, she believes nothing says love like a quilt.

**Lois Lyon**, charter member of Central Oklahoma Quilter's Guild enjoys quilting and friendships made at quilting retreats and workshops.

**Ann McDonald**, married for forty-four years with three children and six grandchildren is currently retired from newspaper writing.

**Linda L. McFadden** is a retired minister and works with older adults. She and her husband Marion have three children, four grandchildren and one great-grandchild. She loves travel and family.

**Chalise Miner** writes for magazines and newspapers, has led writing groups and workshops in Oklahoma, Kansas and Colorado. She is the author of *Rain Forest Girl* and is working on a mainstream novel, *The House on Cherry Street,* and *Long River Home,* a historical novel.

**Linda Morton's** mother taught her to sew in the fourth grade. Linda has been seriously quilting for the last sixteen years.

**Vicki Potts**, elementary teacher, is the daughter of the late, well-loved quilter, author and teacher, Sharon Newman. Vicki and her husband, Gary, have two daughters and are members of Central Baptist Church in Marshall, TX.

**Judith Ann Qurazzo**, born in 1942, dedicated her life and time to her three children and is now enjoying her grandkids.

**Rhonda Richards** graduated Phi Beta Kappa from Birmingham-Southern College with a double major in English and history. An avid quilter, she has edited more than a dozen quilting publications and now works as a copy editor for a national magazine.

**Carolyn Rowe** from Bethany, OK has a counseling practice in Sugar Land, TX after completing her Masters Degree in Counseling from Liberty University. She misses her mom's encouragement and prayers.

**Gerry Snyder**, eighty-four, of Lake Jackson, TX, loves quilting on the solid maple quilt frame her husband of sixty-five years made for her. Needlework and quilting have always been an important part of her life.

**Beverly Sievers** loves teaching longarm quilting after retiring from John Deere Tractor Works in Waterloo, IA. She taught her grandchildren to quilt at her summer Grandma Camp.

**M. Carolyn Steele** has won numerous writing awards, is published in several anthologies and combines her knowledge of writing and genealogy to present programs on preserving family legends.

**Mary Ann Tate** graduated from OU College of Nursing and worked twenty years as psychiatric nurse. She also had a blues band until she was diagnosed with Myasthenia Gravis which led to quilting while she convalesced.

**Gayla White** has a beautiful daughter, Tiffani, she leads a ministry for single mothers at her church, is a nature photographer, and did the layout and design of *Heavenly Patchwork II.* www.AGlimpsePhotography.com

# *Who is Judy Howard?*

Since 1976, Judy Howard has owned and operated Buckboard Antiques and Quilts in Oklahoma City, Oklahoma.

Her love of quilts developed while taking a class from nationally renowned fiber artist Terrie Mangat. Judy became a charter member of the Oklahoma Quilt Guild, and antique quilts became her specialty.

Julia Roberts, America's sweetheart, likes to give Wedding Ring quilts when her family and friends marry. Jessica Lange and Dustin Hoffman are also celebrity clients, Dustin purchasing seventeen quilts while he was in town filming *Rainman.*

Judy recently moved her shop home to concentrate on her web business. Her mail order business offers photos of 200 antique. You can visit Judy's Website BuckboardQuilts.com to view her online inventory of quality quilts at affordable prices.

Editor Rhonda Richards recently honored Judy by featuring Buckboard Quilts in their boo*k Great American Quilts 2004.* Many of Judy's articles and quilts are showcased in quilt magazines and books.

After graduating in 1966 with honors from Oklahoma Baptist University and doing graduate work at Oklahoma State University, Judy and her husband Bill purchased and operated Howard Equipment Company for ten years. Then, quilting won her heart!

*Heavenly Patchwork* was awarded the Golden Seal as an Oklahoma Centennial Project and one of the stories appears in *Chicken Soup for the Christian Soul II.* OKC Metro Library placed *Heavenly Patchwork* in its Oklahoma Room. Stories won Second and Third Place in the regional OWFI Writing Contest and two Second Places and Honorable Mention in the OCWI Writing Contest.

Judy now presents Historic Quilts of America and Oklahoma History Seen through Quilts, power-point programs, which each include 250 quilts from museums, her collection, and *Heavenly Patchwork.* Judy sponsored the Oklahoma Centennial Quilt Contest for children and adults and offers the collection of 100 winning quilts as a traveling exhibit. She will publish the winners in a book with their stories. She also exhibits Murrah and 911 Memorial Quilts and quilts from *Heavenly Patchwork* at shows, guilds, book signings, libraries, women's clubs, schools, art galleries, museums and churches. To schedule a program, book signing, exhibit, see/purchase her quilts or submit stories call 405-751-3885 or email BuckboardQuilts@cox.net.

# ORDER FORM

Yes, I want _____ copies of *Heavenly Patchwork II* for $14.95 each

| Shipping & Handling: | 1 book | $2.95 |
| | additional books | $1.50 each |
| | 32 books | $14.00 |

| Sales Tax: | Oklahoma Residents | $1.25/book |
| | Canadian orders | 7% GST |

Payment must accompany orders. Allow 2 weeks for delivery.

Supplies are limited, so order today!

For an excellent Fund-Raiser, I will donate 50% of the cost to your nonprofit Quilt Guild, Church or group:

Order 32 books @ $7.95/each = $254.40 + 14.00 = $268.40
Order 64 books @ $7.50/each = $480.00 + 28.00 = $508.00
Order 96 books @ $6.95/each = $667.20 + 42.00 = $709.20

My check or money order for $_____ for ___ books is enclosed

Name_____

Organization_____

Address_____

City/State/Zip_____

Phone_____ Email_____

For questions call 405-751-3885
Make your check payable and return to:
Dorcas Publishing
12101 N. MacArthur, Suite 137
Oklahoma City, OK  73162-1800
www.HeavenlyPatchwork.com

*Heavenly Patchwork II---182*